TEN LORDS A LEAPING

Twelve Days of Christmas

Emily E K Murdoch

DRAGONBLADE PUBLISHING, INC.

ARE YOU SIGNED UP FOR DRAGONBLADE'S BLOG?

You'll get the latest news and information on exclusive giveaways, exclusive excerpts, coming releases, sales, free books, cover reveals and more.

Check out our complete list of authors, too!

No spam, no junk. That's a promise!

Sign Up Here

www.dragonbladepublishing.com

Dearest Reader;

Thank you for your support of a small press. At Dragonblade Publishing, we strive to bring you the highest quality Historical Romance from some of the best authors in the business. Without your support, there is no 'us', so we sincerely hope you adore these stories and find some new favorite authors along the way.

Happy Reading!

CEO, Dragonblade Publishing

Additional Dragonblade books by Author Emily E K Murdoch

Twelve Days of Christmas
Twelve Drummers Drumming
Eleven Pipers Piping
Ten Lords a Leaping
Nine Ladies Dancing

The De Petras Saga
The Misplaced Husband (Book 1)
The Impoverished Dowry (Book 2)
The Contrary Debutante (Book 3)
The Determined Mistress (Book 4)
The Convenient Engagement (Book 5)

The Governess Bureau Series
A Governess of Great Talents (Book 1)
A Governess of Discretion (Book 2)
A Governess of Many Languages (Book 3)
A Governess of Prodigious Skill (Book 4)
A Governess of Unusual Experience (Book 5)
A Governess of Wise Years (Book 6)
A Governess of No Fear (Novella)

Never The Bride Series
Always the Bridesmaid (Book 1)
Always the Chaperone (Book 2)
Always the Courtesan (Book 3)
Always the Best Friend (Book 4)
Always the Wallflower (Book 5)
Always the Bluestocking (Book 6)
Always the Rival (Book 7)
Always the Matchmaker (Book 8)

Always the Widow (Book 9)
Always the Rebel (Book 10)
Always the Mistress (Book 11)
Always the Second Choice (Book 12)
Always the Mistletoe (Novella)
Always the Reverend (Novella)

The Lyon's Den Connected World
Always the Lyon Tamer

Pirates of Britannia Series
Always the High Seas

De Wolfe Pack: The Series
Whirlwind with a Wolfe

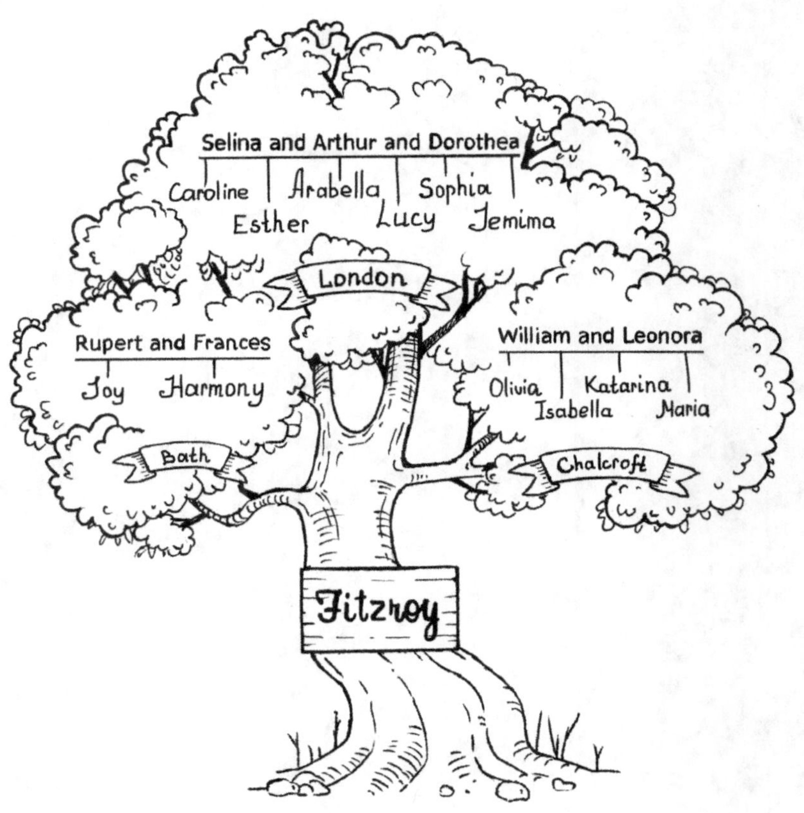

Selina and Arthur and Dorothea
Caroline
Esther
Arabella
Lucy
Sophia
Jemima
London
Rupert and Frances
Joy
Harmony
Bath
William and Leonora
Olivia
Isabella
Katarina
Maria
Chalcroft
Fitzroy

CHAPTER ONE

CAROLINE GASPED AS Stuart gently eased her gown down over her shoulders.

"Stuart…" Her voice was quiet, his name soft on her lips. "Stuart, we shouldn't…"

He smiled. A trickle of light fell onto his face through the curtains in his lodgings, which they had closed to keep out the winter sun, to keep out the prying world.

Her heart raced. This was wrong; they should have been at the Assembly Rooms an hour ago. Yet she had no wish to leave. No desire to end this moment.

The sight of her shoulders made Stuart sigh appreciatively. "Caroline, you are so beautiful…"

They were lying on the bed facing each other, the tops of her breasts uncovered. A faint hint of her nipples appeared each time she took a deep breath.

Her hair was loose, spread across the white pillow like fire on snow. She watched Stuart swallow, clenching his hands as he fought the temptation to rip her gown off, displaying her in all her glory.

He did not need to say the words for her to know it. She knew his every thought, his every movement. His every desire.

Caroline reached out a hand, slowly unbuttoning the waistcoat that was all there was between her fingers and his shirt. Her breath caught in her throat as she heard the muffled breath of her lover. Stuart Walsingham.

This was a routine they had played out many times in their courtship, months of being genteel in public and trying desperately not to consummate the passion they felt for each other in private.

A passion that only grew with each passing day. It was becoming unbearable, the tension between her legs, the heightened sensations they indulged in during those few moments alone they were able to find.

Caroline licked her lips before she spoke, and she watched Stuart's gaze follow the movement. "Stuart, you have been courting me for months—"

"Several long months," interjected Stuart with a smile.

The smile was returned. "And in that time, we have been, for want of a better word, good," Caroline continued. Her breathing quickened as Stuart brushed his fingertips over her collarbone and across her shoulder. "Stuart, I'm talking…"

"And I am not stopping you," said Stuart, his eyes fixed on her face, not on the delicate path that his fingers were taking near her décolletage.

Caroline's concentration flickered as she tried simultaneously to lose herself in the delicious sensation and to concentrate enough to speak.

It was wonderful. He was wonderful. Everything he did to her was glorious, was so close to what she wanted, and yet always stopped right when he was about to…

"You know," she said in a hushed and trembling voice, "you know that we should not…"

She raised her hand, splaying it across Stuart's abdomen, feeling the taut muscles, his desire to crush her to him.

Stuart groaned under his breath as her exploratory fingers moved over his shirt and went to undo his buttons—anything to get his flesh closer to hers.

"No," whispered Caroline, batting his fingers away, "I get to decide how much of these we remove, thank you. That was the agreement."

She had not thought such an agreement would ever be so tested when she had first met the charming young doctor at—whose dinner was it? She could no longer remember.

She could remember how she had felt when Dr. Walsingham had first bowed and taken her hand to dance. A shiver of pleasure, heat, unexpected. The longing to see him again, immediately.

The agreement had been decided upon within weeks of meeting. Their desire then was unbridled, unhidden from each other.

And it was simple: She set the pace. Caroline decided what happened, what was removed, where she was touched…

And that was that.

"Can't I choose how much of this we remove?" Stuart countered, his smile mirroring hers. With deft fingers, he had untied the bows resting between her breasts, and they spilled out.

Caroline gasped, but the expected shame did not follow.

Nothing she did with Stuart felt wrong. None of their kisses, their quick fumbles at the back of a dancehall, the way his fingers entwined with hers, promising pleasures and delights that they had not yet explored.

The delicate ecstasy he had given her that they kept promising they would never do again…

Stuart seemed unable to hold back any longer. He pushed himself forward and kissed her, ready and waiting for him. His tongue tangled with hers, and she sighed with pleasure into his mouth.

Stuart's hand rested on the small of her back as he devoured her lips. Then her collarbones, her neck, her décolletage, and finally her breasts he seemed ravenous for. His teeth scraped across one of her nipples, and Caroline arched her back into him.

"Oh, Stuart!" she murmured, her fingers weaving into his hair. "We mustn't—"

"Hang mustn't!" Stuart said as he nuzzled her neck, pushing her so that she lay flat on the bed facing up at him.

One quick move had him nestled between her legs, and Caroline squirmed with pleasure to feel the hardness of him pushing up against her once more.

"I spend all day longing for these moments," she confided, smiling up at the man that she loved. "All day. All week."

Stuart grinned, though it was difficult to restrain themselves. Even though her skirts and his breeches kept them apart, they both knew what was just out of reach, what they had not permitted themselves to do, things they had not yet explored.

Caroline hastily unbuttoned his shirt, pulling it off and throwing it to the carpet—another line they had never before crossed. Overcome with emotion, she found she no longer wished to dance along the line they had set for themselves.

Far more fun to push past it, desperate for his touch, desperate for all of him.

They both quivered at the intensity of being pressed skin to skin.

"God, Stuart," Caroline murmured.

"I know."

He dipped his face to hers, and their kisses intensified as Caroline ran her hands up and down his back. As he went to suckle hard on her nipples, Caroline moaned and accidentally scraped his back with her nails, causing Stuart to thrust his hips against hers.

Caroline knew what would happen if they were discovered.

No vouchers to Almack's would ever be issued to a young lady who was known to be tupped, even if it was by a gentleman courting her.

Men could have all the fun, but ladies? Ladies were meant to be pure.

Caroline did not feel pure right now. Each kiss Stuart lavished on her felt like hot wax falling on her skin. Especially on that delicate spot just above her nipples that made her shudder as his kisses intensified.

Her fingers moved from Stuart's back to his chest, scattered with the same light brown curly hair that covered his head. Caroline swallowed as her gaze trailed down below his stomach to—

She could not help herself.

Ever since she had laid eyes on Stuart, she had felt a stirring in her stomach and below in her secret place.

There was something so distinctly animalistic about him. The way he held himself, so taut, so ready to pounce at any moment. The smile that he bestowed on her that first day was dazzling, and she had been captivated by his light ever since.

Inseparable, the center of much gossip—an engagement expected—that did not prevent Caroline and Stuart from sharing every experience together that they possibly could.

At first, they were hesitant, but as the certainty of their mutual feelings slowly became clear, there was nothing to prevent them from enjoying picnics, card games, balls, afternoon gatherings, everything that they could—with chaperones present, of course.

Caroline gasped as Stuart drew one of her legs up around him, then pulling himself closer to her. His fingers on her thigh felt like fire, and she gloried in the sensation.

"Caroline." Stuart spoke her name in a ragged voice that easily betrayed his emotion.

It was wonderful to be so desired, to hear the desperation in his voice. She arched herself into him and found her fingers clutching at the button at the top of his breeches.

There was a sharp intake of breath, and Stuart pulled her fingers away.

Caroline stared at him, eyes hazy with desire. "Why are you stopping me?"

Stuart was breathing heavily.

"Not again, Caroline, you know that." He swallowed, obviously troubled.

She looked up at him, knowing he was right but unable to deny the feelings growing inside her, the ache that had not yet been satisfied. "But I want—"

"I know," interjected Stuart with a knowing smile. "Trust me, if anyone knows how you feel right now, it is I!" He pushed his hand through his hair. "But if those come off, I am telling you, I will make love to you. I won't be able to stop at just touching, not again."

Caroline squirmed at the thought of him possessing her completely.

Stuart groaned as she shuddered against his hardness.

"You know that I am right," he said in a pleading tone.

STUART KNEW WHAT he should do; he should step away from the beautiful, tempting, half-naked woman on his bed.

But he didn't. Of course.

He was a man, not a statue! Though now he came to think of it, some parts of him were rock hard…

Stuart attempted a steadying breath as he lay nestled between Caroline's thighs. Damn and blast, but he should be given a medal for preventing her from undoing his breeches. Her innocence—at least, technically—was just about intact, and he should be praised for that.

He itched to place his hands once more on those beautiful breasts mere inches from his palms, but he knew he was close to losing the control he had fought to keep for several weeks.

Looking back, he should have known.

Stuart should have known sneaking Caroline up the backstairs of his lodgings—carefully avoiding his landlady—to play card games and read together was a mistake. Now that they had a place to go, just the two of them with no chaperone, they had quickly broken all of Society's rules—and reveled in the pleasure they found together.

But no more. He had to stop.

Caroline reached up for one of Stuart's hands. "I know that you are right," she whispered, bringing his hand to her lips and bestowing a kiss right in the center of his palm. "My head knows it," she continued, starting to place kisses on his fingertips between words. Stuart said nothing but felt the twitch of his hardness with every soft, fluttering kiss, "and my heart knows it—yet unfortunately, my body does not feel it. It feels something quite different."

Her eyes darkened with desire, and she slowly yet steadily moved Stuart's hand across her breast—which he tried to caress—past her stomach, and moving her skirts up with her other hand, brought his hand right down to her secret place.

"Please," she murmured, looking up at him with desperation. "You know what I want."

"Christ, Caroline," Stuart swore under his breath as his fingers unconsciously wandered across the warm curls beneath them, feeling the wetness of her desire.

They had attempted to promise each other that they would never do this again.

To hear her cry out his name... Stuart closed his eyes as he forced his hands to splay on her waist, rather than fumble with the buttons of his breeches.

This was the best way. She wanted pleasure. He would give her pleasure.

Caroline gasped and closed her eyes as Stuart's fingers gently stroked.

It reminded him of the first time they had traversed this line. She had never done anything that bold before, and it was Stuart who had initiated the passion between them and introduced her to the delights of touch.

But now she tempted him beyond the limitations they had previously set—and Stuart found himself utterly captivated by her.

How could he not be? More beautiful than the whole of Society put together, more wit than any lady he had ever known, and a desire for pleasure that matched his own.

The perfect woman.

Stuart lowered himself toward Caroline again, his hand remaining exactly where it was, concentrating on making sure he did not rush things. That was important. If she was to enjoy the very best of his fingers, he could not rush her.

He kissed her again, tasting the lust on her tongue.

Nothing else mattered, nothing else existed beyond the four walls of this room, beyond the bed.

Stuart finally surrendered to his cravings. His mouth returned to her lips, hushing her whimpers.

Caroline threw her head back as her breath shortened, her hands twisted into Stuart's hair as her love's fingers gently worked.

Stuart shuddered as he tried to control his breathing. Caroline felt so wonderful, so perfect around his fingers. The gentle rhythm he was beating started to increase and he could sense the change in her, and it was torture to be this close to her without delving his manhood into her warmth.

He had to stop himself from doing what he would later regret.

"Stuart," cried Caroline softly as he built the pressure within her, as the pleasure started to increase beyond what she could stand, "Stuart, more—"

But he stopped her mouth with a fervent kiss to silence her as his hands brought her to climax.

This was what he wanted, though he had fought against his feelings for propriety's sake. Not just genteel Caroline, the one everyone else saw.

He craved the secret Caroline. *This Caroline.*

Her cries finally subsided. Caroline went weak and limp, and Stuart lay beside her, trying his best to think ice cold thoughts as his manhood struggled against his breeches.

"That was…" Caroline's voice was a mere flutter, but Stuart's ears were well accustomed to hearing her across a crowded room. "I mean…Stuart…"

Stuart swallowed, willing his desire to pass. "I know," he managed.

They held each other in silence for a few moments, then Stuart pushed himself up and off the bed.

Caroline's eyes were still partially closed. "Stuart?"

Stuart smiled. Though the carpet on the floor of his lodgings was thin and rather injurious to the knee, he did not mind. He knelt by the bed, a box in his hands—a box that was open. Within it sat a very large diamond attached to a band of gold.

Caroline's mouth opened in surprise.

It was precisely the reaction Stuart had hoped for. A young doctor took time to build up a list of patients, and he had…well, so little to offer Caroline.

But the thought of living without her…

"Stuart," she said, sitting up with her legs over the side of the bed, facing him. "What—"

"Miss Caroline Fitzroy," said Stuart, obviously nervous. "You are the most wonderful and fascinating person I have ever met. Every day I spend more time with you, I am further amazed. Each conversation proves you to be more precious. Each moment we share convinces me there is no one else that I would rather spend the rest of my life with."

Caroline did not blush; how could she, after what they had just shared? But it was evidently not a speech she had been expecting.

Stuart swallowed. There was no one else for him but Caroline, and she would surely not have indulged in such pleasure with him if she did not intend to be his wife. This was right. This was going to make them both so happy.

"Miss Caroline Fitzroy," Stuart continued, raising the box with the ring toward her, "will you do me the incredible honor of agreeing to become my wife?"

CHAPTER TWO

THE SILENCE HAD continued too long.

Stuart coughed, heart skipping a beat. "Caroline?"

"I heard you," she said slowly, her eyes fixed on the ring in the box in his hand. "I am just…thinking."

Rising from the floor, Stuart sat next to Caroline on the bed. "I am attempting not to be offended by the length of time your thinking requires, but I must inform you the battle could be short-lived," he said jovially, his smile fading as he received no response. "Caroline?"

There was no response. Panic started to twist in his stomach. "Can…can you hear me?"

She nodded.

Finally, her gaze moved from the box to his eyes, and Stuart was somewhat relieved to discover there was still warmth in her expression.

"For a moment there, I thought that you were going to refuse me," he said quietly.

Caroline smiled nervously. "I have not decided either way."

Stuart's eyes widened in shock. "Either way? Caroline, I love you. You love me—we love each other, we have done for the best part of a year. Each time we are together, I can tell you, try to show you—when we kiss—"

"Desire is not the same as love!" Caroline rose, leaving Stuart seated alone on the bed. "Can you not see how we could be influenced when it comes to our emotions, when we engage in…" The left shoulder of her gown had slipped down, revealing her breast. She had not tied the ribbons, and she pulled it up irritably. "You know what I mean. Besides, your mother hates me."

"She doesn't hate you."

"She doesn't like me."

Stuart opened his mouth, hesitated, then said, "You believe I propose only to make love to you, as I have wished for many weeks?"

"Well," said Caroline hesitantly. "Yes. Perhaps."

Stuart sighed, rose from the bed, and walked over to his desk by the window.

There were many books and papers, most of them medical in nature. Dr. Stuart Walsingham was, after all, a rising star in the world of medicine.

Two or three empty ink bottles lay on the desk alongside a broken quill and a wad of sealing wax that had been scraped from letters he had received. Every shilling saved was one earned.

There was a letter there from his mother that he should have replied to by now. She would be arriving in London any day, and these murmurs of "important news" were starting to get repetitive. What on earth could she possibly need to tell him?

"It's from your mother, isn't it?"

Stuart smiled ruefully as he turned to look at her. "How did you know?"

"You only get that look," Caroline said darkly, "when thinking about your mother. She still disapproves of me."

"I cannot possibly think why," Stuart muttered. "You're perfect, Caroline, and her talk of you not being good enough for—"

"I beg your pardon?"

"It's your parents who need to give permission, not mine," Stuart said hastily. Time to get back on track; the last thing he needed was to give Caroline further reasons to decline him.

She was smiling, though the smile was a little dejected. Stuart's heart twisted. Damn his mother for being so infuriating!

"Caroline," he said gently, without reproof, "it saddens me that you believe I would rashly encourage you into anything you are not comfortable with, including a proposal of marriage."

Caroline sighed. "It is not that I do not trust you, nor believe you have malevolent intent," she said softly. "It is more…it is easy to be swept along by one's passions. Acting on the spur of the moment is not the best way to enter into an engagement to be married."

Stuart laughed quietly. *Oh, he would have her, and soon. All he longed for…* "My darling love, do you honestly think a man can just simply lay his hand on a diamond ring whenever the thought springs upon him?"

Caroline's eyes darted toward the box, now closed, on his desk.

"Caroline, I bought that ring a month ago," said Stuart matter-of-factly, "and I knew well before then there was only one person I wished to spend my life with. This felt like the perfect moment."

Caroline's smile began to return, her eyes lighting up. "You— you mean to say that ring is truly an engagement ring? That is a rather extravagant new fashion to follow, is it not?"

She did not say, *for a man of your means,* and Stuart pushed the thought away. She had not meant it that way, surely.

"I can afford it," he said stiffly.

Caroline arched an eyebrow. "This mysterious benefactor? I still do not understand why you are not more curious about this unknown person who has supported you financially."

"Still supports me," Stuart said, his voice becoming harsh despite his best efforts. "My mother refuses to share any details, only that he wished to see me established. I imagine if he changed his mind, he would withdraw that support!"

He should not have spoken. A flicker of concern rushed across Caroline's features. "Truly? You could be cut off so swiftly?"

Instead, he shrugged. "Perhaps, and I suppose you will say that spending this money on a ring is a poor decision!"

"Well, you'll have my three thousand pounds," said Caroline lightly.

Stuart tried not to wince again. Three thousand pounds. A fortune, as far as he was concerned. "You know I love you for yourself, not your dowry."

"I do."

"And an engagement ring was rather an extravagance," he admitted. "But it is a trend I like, and matters not who in the *ton* is follows it and who shuns it. I like the idea of you having my promise resting on your finger, for you to smile at when we are apart. I had hoped you would find it pleasing."

He had not intended to sound petulant, but the disappointment of not receiving a resounding affirmative to his proposal still rankled in Stuart's heart.

He pushed aside the bitterness. Had not Caroline explained precisely her hesitation? *Could he blame her, really?*

His hand reached for the box, and opening it, passed it to Caroline.

Covered and lined with velvet, a deep blue that threw the gold of the band into glorious relief, it looked cumbersome in her hand.

The diamond was indeed large. Stuart had been most insistent to the insolent boy at the jewelers that nothing could compare to Caroline's beauty, but they had endeavored to find a ring to do her justice.

Now he saw her with it, Stuart knew he had made the right decision. The pearl ring he had been tempted by, though elegant, was nothing to the glitter of the diamond. It had taken every shilling he could find, and agreeing to care for a few patients with payments in advance, something he had never been brave enough to request.

His mother considered engagement rings to be crass. Perhaps

they were. Perhaps it was just her inexplicable dislike of Caroline.

All Stuart knew was that he wanted the world to know how he loved her. That she was his, and that she rested under his protection. That Caroline Fitzroy would not keep her name much longer.

As she twisted the box in her hand, sunlight was caught in the diamond, throwing a rainbow around the room and across Stuart's face.

"Do you…do you like it?"

Caroline beamed, taking the ring out of the box and placing it on the fourth finger of her left hand. "Like it? I adore it—much as I adore the man who gave it to me."

Relief, sweet relief, rushed through him.

He had really believed for a moment there that she was going to refuse him.

How would he ever have been able to face anyone once the news got out—and it would do, these things always were known eventually—that the eldest Miss Fitzroy had refused him?

Stuart leaned forward to take her hand.

"And now," he said quietly, "I would very much like to re-move every item of clothing from your body, save that ring, and continue to bring you pleasure all afternoon—but," Stuart said quickly, noting the delight that flashed across Caroline's face, "we shall instead go and see your family. It is high time your father knew I have acted upon my promise to him."

"YOUR… YOUR PROMISE to him?" Caroline's voice was full of confusion.

She was not that old, surely, that her father had to draw promises from young men to propose matrimony, was she?

Her betrothed—and how wonderful to think of Stuart that way, as a delicious thrill passed through her body—picked up the shirt he had removed. He tutted to find several buttons pulled loose in their passion.

"When I asked him permission to marry you, the day before I found the ring," Stuart answered. "You do not think I would approach you with such overtures without ascertaining that your father was happy with my suit? Besides, is not your family expecting us for dinner?"

Caroline smiled as she watched him continue to dress, chuckling to himself.

She had never met anyone who was so intelligent as Stuart, no one who truly enjoyed the company of others. There was something noble about him, something that drew her to him.

She was a fortunate woman. She knew it, watching him carefully button his shirt over a tight stomach that promised such delights as her eyes roved downward…

Caroline swallowed. *She really needed to concentrate.* She was going to spend the rest of her life truly exploring and appreciating his character.

"Caroline?"

She had become lost in her thoughts. It took him repeating her name a few times before she realized Stuart was standing before her, fully clothed and wearing his greatcoat with her pelisse in his outstretched hand.

His smile widened. "Shall we?"

"Goodness, I do apologize, Stuart," said Caroline, quickly fiddling with the ribbon at the front of her gown and tying it into a large bow as she rose from the bed. "I must admit I quite forgot myself!"

She had barely regained her balance when Stuart placed a hand on her behind and pulled her close.

"And if you are not careful, Miss Fitzroy, I shall forget myself, and we shall miss your family dinner," he breathed into her ear.

Every part of Caroline wanted to melt into a pool at his feet. Surely now they were engaged to be married, it would not be so wrong to permit themselves the ultimate pleasure, would it?

Caroline swallowed and looked into Stuart's dancing eyes. It appeared he could see precisely what she was thinking. What she wanted. What she knew he could give her.

She took a deep breath and felt the weight of the diamond ring on her finger.

"Come now," she said, gently pushing away from him and smiling at his irrepressible grin. "If you are truly to announce this to my family, let us go."

As they almost ran down the backstairs, Stuart had the presence of mind to call out to his landlady that he would be dining with the Fitzroys, and then they were out the door and into the street.

It was not a complete accident that Stuart Walsingham had chosen lodgings only ten minutes' walk from the Fitzroy London address. Caroline took Stuart's arm, and they began to walk in the chilly November air. There was ice on the ground and snow had not fallen yet—but the gossip in London was that it would arrive that very evening.

"It is a shame Esther and Lucy are in Bath with our cousins," said Caroline with a sigh as they dodged a woman trying to sell rather grubby looking lace. "I would much rather have told all my sisters at the same time—they will be disappointed to hear the news from a letter."

"That is a shame," said Stuart, "but I am afraid I did not consider your many sisters' whereabouts within my proposal plans!"

Caroline laughed, her cheeks flushing at the remembrance of his proposal; Stuart without his shirt, her gown only half tied, heat still flowing through her body as the echoes of pleasure rippled through her body.

"Especially," said Stuart with a laugh, "with five sisters, orchestrating something between the six Fitzroy girls is something of an impossibility."

They crossed the road as he spoke, and Caroline waited until they had reached the other side safely before protesting, "I do not know what you consider so impossible!"

"I know you have explained it all to me before," said Stuart with a sigh. "Let me see if I can recall accurately. Your mother was a widow with yourself and Esther, she met Mr. Fitzroy who was a widower with Jemima, and they proceeded to have three more daughters."

"Arabella, Lucy, and Sophia," said Caroline promptly with a mischievous grin. "I do not know why you find it so complicated."

Stuart threw his arms up to the sky in mock exhaustion. "There are six of you! The entire brood is something of a mix between chaos and friendship. I admit myself rather impressed at how calm your father always seemed to be, surrounded by seven women!"

A gaggle of newspaper hawkers, all attempting to outdo the other, at the next street corner muffled their conversation with shouts of murders, political intrigues, and shipping disasters.

Caroline did not attempt to speak until they had continued a little farther down the road. "Do not fear, I was not suggesting we delay telling my family—more I shall have to write a letter before Papa's reaches Uncle Rupert!"

"Now, he is your father's brother, is that correct?" Stuart creased his forehead in concentration. "You must forgive me, Caroline," he said after they both hopped over a large pile of horse droppings that had somehow made its way onto the pavement, "you know my own family is small, and I cannot fathom how you follow your own!"

Tightening her arm in his, Caroline laughed. "Really Stuart, 'tis not so complex! Papa is one of three brothers: the eldest, William, lives at Chalcroft, which is the family seat with his wife and four daughters, and the middle brother, Rupert, dwells in Bath with his wife and two daughters."

Stuart shook his head sadly. "Twelve of you in total!"

Twelve Fitzroy cousins. *Goodness, there were rather a lot of them.* Caroline had never thought about it that way.

"It is rather a lot, I suppose," she said thoughtfully as they turned onto her street. "Yet having six cousins has never felt numerous. I suppose because I have so many sisters of my own to start with."

"Well, even if you had two cousins," said Stuart, stopping with his bride-to-be outside her front door, "I do not think I would be any closer to following your family tree than now!"

Caroline tapped him playfully on the arm, then leaned forward to ring the bell. "You are not truly intimidated, are you?"

It had never occurred to her. Her family was…her family. Complex, rowdy, usually with something dramatic occurring at all times… *the Fitzroys*. It had never struck her that they could be any other way.

"Intimidated?" repeated Stuart.

Caroline glanced up at him. There was a certain line that always appeared on his forehead when he was attempting to sound more impressive than he was; it was one of those little quirks she loved about him.

She could see it now.

"Although my feelings and intentions toward you were serious early in their courtship," Stuart said quietly, "the thought of declaring to your tight knit family that I am about to take away one of their precious daughters, their most beautiful jewel in my opinion… no, that does not make me feel easy."

Caroline's eyes filled with concern, but Stuart was unable to say more before the front door swung open and Mrs. Castle, the Fitzroys' housekeeper, stood before them.

"Oh, Miss Caroline!" Mrs. Castle spoke with surprise. "The master said you would not return home directly after attending the Assembly Rooms. Whatever have you been up to!"

An undoubtedly scarlet flush covered her cheeks as Caroline tried to ignore heady thoughts of what she had been up to. Her engagement, that was what she should be thinking of—and the temptation to tell the housekeeper, who had been with the family so long, even before she saw her parents, overwhelmed her.

How was she supposed to keep it all in? How did anyone keep such a thing a secret, when all she wanted to do was shout it from the rooftops?

"Do not worry, Mrs. Castle, nothing is wrong. Is everyone at home?"

Mrs. Castle stood back so Caroline and Stuart could step in out of the cold. "Master and mistress are in the drawing room, with Miss Jemima, Miss Arabella, and Miss Sophia."

"Excellent," said Stuart as he shrugged off his greatcoat. "Oh no, Mrs. Castle," he said smoothly as she tried to take it from him. "Do let me—I am sure you have much to do."

"As you wish, sir," she said good naturedly, her particular approval for the gentleman clear to see. "I will see to dinner."

Stuart bowed as Mrs. Castle bustled off back to the kitchen to oversee her staff. Caroline watched him visibly relax as he helped her remove her pelisse.

"You…you are nervous, aren't you, Stuart?" Caroline would never have thought it possible. "I mean, you're a doctor! You have people's lives in your hands every day!"

"Not exactly nervous, no," he said quietly. "Excited. I am about to finally announce to the world something I have wanted to say for a very long time. I love Miss Caroline Fitzroy—and more, she loves me, too, and is about to become my wife."

Caroline could not restrain herself. She leaned forward and kissed him firmly on his lips. *How could she help it?* Such a handsome man, such a kind man—all her own.

Her arms moved to encircle him, but Stuart caught her wrists with a deep and quiet laugh.

"You know exactly what will happen if we start to do that, and the last thing I want is for your father to remove his blessing by finding me out here in the corridor with you pushed up against a wall."

His voice was low, but Caroline caught every word. A quiet moan escaped from her mouth. How was he so controlled?

Taking her hand in his, Stuart pulled her lightly to stand before the door of the drawing room. It bore a wreath of holly, and a quick look upward revealed a bunch of mistletoe hanging from the ceiling.

"Ready?" Stuart whispered.

Caroline nodded, heart pounding. Her Papa had given his permission, Stuart had said, and her mother would be naught but raptures to hear the news.

So why did this moment suddenly fill her with foreboding, as though something would occur to wrench away the man she loved?

Stuart reached out his hand, the one not entwined with her own, and opened the door.

Mrs. Castle had been busy here, decorating the Fitzroy house for Advent. It was, after all, Advent Sunday. Red candles with gold ribbons were scattered around the room. There was holly and ivy on the mantelpiece and over the paintings on the walls, and the whole room looked beautiful.

Caroline had only seen it that morning, and no decorations from what she could see had been added, but it looked more beautiful, more decadent than she remembered.

Was this what true happiness did? Beautified everything around her?

"Dr. Walsingham!" It was her Papa who had spoken as he rose from sitting beside her stepsister, Jemima—a woman who looked most disgruntled, although Caroline could not for the life of her comprehend why.

A quick glance around the room revealed Sophia and Arabella seated at the other end of the room with their mother around a table, cards in their hands. Aside from Jemima, there were smiles everywhere.

"Caroline, you did not inform us that you would be returning early," her mother Selina said, beaming. "You sly thing!"

"I hope nothing is the matter," said Arabella with concern, a frown furrowing into the delicate flame-red curls framing her forehead. "You have not taken ill, Caroline?"

"If she had, she would hardly come here, would she? Not as she was already with the great doctor."

Caroline saw Stuart wince at Jemima's sarcastic tone out of the corner of her eye. Arabella blushed but continued to smile, while the youngest, Sophia, looked between the sisters with confusion.

Taking a deep breath, Caroline reminded herself Jemima was always this bad tempered. It had nothing to do with her. *Probably*.

Arthur, her Papa, opened up his arms as he spoke. "Come on in then, you two," he said jovially. "Take a seat and join us for the evening."

Caroline was about to accept her stepfather's offer, yet her hand was held within Stuart's, keeping her from moving forward.

"If it acceptable to you, sir," said Stuart, his voice level, "I would rather remain here, standing, while I speak to you all for a moment."

Sophia looked up from her cards, placing them in the lap of her violently orange gown which clashed horribly with her beautiful red hair.

"Then speak," said her Papa, seating himself once more.

Stuart cleared his throat, and Caroline felt such a swell of love for him that she took his hand and brought it around her waist. The simple gesture, calmly done without ceremony, seemed to bring Stuart back to the moment.

"Mr. Fitzroy, Mrs. Fitzroy, ladies," he began, his voice strengthening. "You know I have been courting your daughter and sister Caroline for many months now. They have been the happiest times of my life, and I am afraid that I am very unwilling to part with her each time that I return her to you."

As he spoke, Caroline looked around the room. It appeared no one had guessed what Stuart was about to announce.

Why should they? It had certainly been a surprise to her, though she had wished for it, of course.

Then she caught a knowing smile from her stepfather, and flushed. Well, of course he knew. Had not Stuart said he had asked his permission?

Caroline glanced at her mother and saw tears already forming in the corners of her eyes. Ah. So, her mother knew, too.

That meant it would only be a surprise to her sisters and she could already guess what their responses would be…

"And so, we would like to announce that we are engaged to be married!"

Gasps echoed through the room, and then her Papa stood up to clap his future son-in-law on the back. Her mother rose from her chair, and with her came Arabella and Sophia.

"Engaged!" cried her mother, reaching up a hand to push back a curl of wild red hair sliced with silver which had escaped her pins. "My little Caroline engaged to be married!"

Caroline barely knew where to look, whom to speak with first—yet could not help but notice Jemima had not risen, ignoring the news completely.

"The first Fitzroy wedding! Goodness me!" cried their father, wringing Stuart's hand. "I shall have to hope you do not all wish to marry in the same Season, or I shall be ruined!"

Joy rushed through Caroline's heart as her Papa moved to the fireplace to speak with her Mama. She was so happy, but more, she had made her family so happy. What woman could ask for more?

She was attempting to listen to her family's overtures when Stuart leaned toward her ear and whispered, "You know, I have much respect and admiration for your family… yet I would rather be doing what we were an hour ago."

Heat blossomed from where Stuart's breath touched her ear. Caroline unconsciously brought her hand to it as though expecting it to be scalding hot.

"Stuart!" she whispered quietly, but Sophia was still talking, and it was clear no one else had heard his remark.

The smile on his face told her he was secure in the knowledge he would not be found out.

Caroline could not help but smile. *This was really happening,* she thought as she tried desperately to pay attention to her sister. *I am really engaged. Engaged to be married to Dr Stuart Walsingham.*

Mrs. Walsingham.

"And he is such a handsome man," her mother was saying, causing blushes in both Caroline and Stuart's cheeks. "Very handsome, though I do say so myself."

"Mama!"

"I saw it all coming, of course, it was obvious," said Arabella with a smile.

Caroline breathed a sigh of relief. Her peacemaking sister. Thank goodness she had cut across their mother to halt her embarrassing remarks!

"We'll be married by Easter, if I have my way," said Stuart, squeezing his hand around Caroline's waist. "If not sooner!"

Caroline laughed at his nonsense as her sisters joined with her laughter. Oh, had she ever been as happy as this? Was it possible to be happier?

She could not imagine it. Nothing could take away her joy, nothing at all.

"I wish you had not interrupted my talk with Father," complained Jemima in a frustrated tone. "I have been hoping to speak to him about the war for some time now. Hundreds of people, not just I, have signed it to support our soldiers in the continuing war in France, yet—"

"Again, Jemima?" sighed Caroline. *Why could her stepsister not just halt her nonsense for five minutes together!* Did she have to embarrass them all before Stuart? "We have listened to this time and time again, and still you will not quit your obsession with this war!"

"With peace!" Jemima spoke fervently, hands clasped in her lap. "For it is peace I strive for, and many others across the country! Why should—"

"Jemima, please," said Arabella softly.

Caroline could feel the flush on her cheeks.

It was always the same. Jemima found fault with someone, anyone, and Arabella rushed forward to hastily make amends.

Her stepsister was still muttering about supporting veterans when they returned, but Caroline could not heed her words. Not with Stuart by her side, still graciously accepting the congratulations of her family.

"It is simply too bad poor Esther and Lucy departed not one day before this happy occasion," her Mama said. "They would decide to go to Bath, determined as they were to enjoy all the fashionable treats of the coming Christmas season. They will be with their cousins Joy and Harmony now, though I cannot think the Bath Fitzroys will have news as festive as this!"

None of her daughters were listening.

"Oh, Caroline," breathed Sophia, "it is too much to believe! You and Dr. Walsingham—engaged! Indeed, I cannot believe it!"

That was more like it, thought Caroline approvingly. Though the youngest of the sisters, Sophia always seemed to know what to say. Caroline held out her hand with the glittering diamond ring upon it, as though offering evidence.

"My word!" Sophia reached out to touch her hand, twisting the ring on her fourth finger so it caught more of the candlelight. "Dr. Walsingham has bought you an engagement ring! Only the very finest people are doing so you know, 'tis the height of fashion."

"Only the best," Stuart said grandly, "for the best."

Caroline's smile, if possible, became even broader. *He really was a fool sometimes.* "I had no expectations of such a beautiful jewel, yet it would be remiss of me not to wear it now I have been given it."

Her Papa nodded not at her words, it appeared, but at Stuart's. "It is good to hear you speak so, young Walsingham—I would not have wanted my child to marry anyone who could not value her as she deserves."

Out of the corner of her eye, Caroline saw Arabella join Sophia, and over the conversation between her father and Stuart about current business in town, she could hear snippets of her sisters' conversation—a conversation, it appeared, all about making mischief.

"...we could ensure all the blacksmiths in town are in attendance, or station a large bear near the altar!"

As nonsensical as Sophia's words were, she was so often mischievous it was hardly surprising. Her giggling was so infectious Caroline could not help but chuckle. Who could blame her, on the day the most incredible man asked her to be his wife?

"Champagne, we must have champagne!"

It was all really happening, Caroline had to remind herself as a footman entered the room with seven champagne flutes on a silver tray. After offering them to the happy couple, the servant was inundated by the family as they reached eagerly for their drinks.

But one person had not. One person was still seated in a beautiful crimson gown at the other end of the room, with the most sour and unhappy face Caroline had ever seen. Her sister Jemima.

Caroline tried not to be upset by the irritation she almost always felt whenever Jemima was... well, *Jemima.* She did not wish to look back and remember ire instead of joy.

But surely even *Jemima* could pretend to be happy for her on an occasion such as this?

A mere month apart in age, they were the only Fitzroy daughters who shared no parents. Caroline knew Jemima's mother had died in childbirth, which was terrible, and her own father had died from a fever.

Two tragedies which had brought two families together.

The closeness in their age naturally meant they were often compared, reaching each milestone together or one just behind the other. Despite Caroline's desire to befriend her stepsister, Jemima appeared to feel nothing for her but indifference.

The fact that Jemima was the only Fitzroy sister not to carry Selina's beautiful red hair only meant it was even more obvious that she, with her chestnut hair, was the odd one out.

Caroline's heart twinged. *It could not be easy.*

But that did not mean she could not at least feign congratulations!

Stuart's hand squeezed her own. Caroline blinked. She had been staring into space for a good few minutes. Her mother was now speaking, and she roused her concentration, smile returning.

"With five daughters," her Mama said—a comment that made Caroline wince, as Jemima was sure to take offense at not being included, "it is always a wonderful comfort to myself as a mother to know there are others out there who understand the great beauties that they are. After all, it is the finest day of a mother's life to see her daughter find someone who can make her as happy—nay happier—than her parents. And now this day has come for our eldest child."

Caroline's eyes threatened to fill with tears as her stepfather pulled her mother toward him, and they smiled proudly at her. This was what she had dreamed of—a family so happy—

"Excuse me!"

The family turned to see Jemima standing at the other end of the room, arms crossed so tightly it were as though they had been woven together.

Caroline threw a concerned look at Stuart, who shook his head. He appeared sure Jemima would not make a scene.

How wrong he was.

"I hate to point this out," Jemima said bitterly, taking a step toward them, her crimson gown swishing as she moved, "but *I* am your eldest child."

There was a stunned silence across the room, and Caroline opened her mouth to speak—although exactly what she would have said, she did not quite know. She was not given the chance.

"What you meant to say was that Caroline is *your* eldest child." Jemima may have been the only Fitzroy daughter without the red hair of Selina's children, but she still had the fiery temper. "Papa's eldest child is me."

In the silence that followed, Caroline could hear her mother swallow. Constantly irritable, Jemima was ever ready to explode, and no one wanted to be the person to push her over the edge.

"Well, of course!" Caroline's Mama's voice was low and calm, but there was a slight quiver in it Caroline hoped only she noticed. "You know that is what I meant—"

"Then why didn't you say it?" Jemima's voice cracked as she spoke, and their Papa tightened his arm around his wife. "Papa, I had really wished to speak to you, do you have any time now?"

Their Papa sighed, and Caroline's heart twisted for him. Ever pulled in two directions.

He glanced around at his other daughters. "Naturally, my dear, I will stay a while with Caroline and Dr. Walsingham as—"

"I see." It was a bitter tone that emanated from Jemima's mouth, pain etched across her forehead. "I see now that only if I can bring a gentleman to this house will I be listened to. The fact that thousands of men have perished while we sit here and chatter about how many roses Caroline must have is of no importance. No matter. I shall see myself out."

"No, Jemima, wait—" began her Papa, joined by both Arabella and Sophia in asking her to stay.

Caroline tasted the bitterness in her mouth as she readied herself to ask a question she had no real wish to. She only did so for her Papa—though her stepfather, she had fallen in with her younger half-sisters in calling him Papa, and he was the only father she could remember in any event.

"Stay, Jemima," she said softly.

But Jemima clearly had no such intention. Striding across the room, she pulled open the door before marching through it, leaving it unclosed behind her. The sound of the front door being slammed echoed around the hall and drawing room, then silence returned.

"Ahem." Stuart cleared his throat awkwardly.

Caroline cast him a miserable glance. No wonder he much preferred conversing with Arabella and Esther. It was mortifying to have such hysterics in the family, and after Jemima had seen how it had upset her! Upset them all!

If only Esther and Lucy had been here. Perhaps they would

have been able to reason with Jemima where Arabella could not, though that was a tall order.

Together they kept the peace—most of the time—and Jemima often refrained from fully speaking her mind when Lucy and Sophia were present due to their young ages.

But with two Fitzroy sisters away, Jemima had allowed her fractious feelings to show for all to see, and it had certainly brought an awkward atmosphere into the room.

Caroline felt the tension in her shoulders. *What could she say now?*

"Now then," said her Mama, breaking the silence and reaching for her daughter's hand with a smile, albeit slightly thin. "We are here today to celebrate an exciting marriage, and I declare nothing will distract me from it. Come sit with me, my dear, and we can talk all about it."

Caroline allowed herself to be led to the sofa Jemima had only just recently vacated, and sighed with relief as she sat down.

"Do not worry about her," her mother said in an undertone. Thankfully, Papa and Stuart were starting to talk, Arabella and Sophia joining in occasionally, and covered their own conversation. "She will come back, and she will feel embarrassed and ashamed. Do not fret about her—especially," and here her voice rose, "as you are getting married! Darling, child, how do you feel?"

"I am not entirely sure what I feel at present," said Caroline honestly, an irrepressible smile returning to her face. "I cannot believe it! I mean, I had always hoped my courtship with Stuart—Dr. Walsingham, I mean—would eventually lead me up the aisle, but one never likes to presume. All I could do was hope."

"Hope does not always blossom," said her Mama sagely. "I am so pleased it has ended as I hoped."

Caroline smiled, her gaze falling once more to the large diamond on her finger. Her mother waited a moment or two for her to speak, but she said nothing.

It was all going to change, wasn't it? Her life here, with her parents and her sisters. Their routines, habits, traditions. The way they celebrated Christmas and birthdays and May Day.

It would all be different now.

"Caroline," and now her Mama's voice was serious, "if you are in any way unsure about this—"

"Oh no!" Caroline said hastily, smile returning. "It is not that I doubt myself, nor Dr. Walsingham, nor our feelings for each other. It is more that marriage is such an important thing, so weighty, so important…it is difficult to know exactly what one is to expect."

"Well, every marriage is different." Her mother spoke with frankness, as she always did. "I have been married twice, and there were very few lessons I took from the former into the latter. No man, after all, is quite the same as another."

Caroline looked back across the room to the man who would be her husband. "I will admit I am rather excited to be married."

"Good," said her mother firmly, "and so you should be. If you were not so, I would be counselling you to escape him immediately!"

Their laughter was swiftly interrupted by her Papa. "Caroline?"

She rose and made her way across the room. Stuart held out his hand in welcome, and she happily took it and nestled against him.

"Caroline," her Papa said seriously but with a happy smile. "It would give me great pleasure if you and your fine young gentleman would give me your permission to hold a ball in your honor—an engagement ball, if you will."

"Sir, it is we who are honored," said Stuart. Caroline shivered as she felt the vibration of his voice through her body. "It would give us nothing but pleasure. Regretfully, a note has arrived from one of my patients, I must depart—"

Irritation curled around Caroline's heart, though she pushed it aside. This was going to be her life: she would be the wife of a doctor. She would have to become accustomed to him departing so swiftly.

"No worries, my boy, off with you!" Caroline's father said good naturedly. "What a nice young man."

"Thank you, Papa," said Caroline quietly.

She was not one given to effusions of praise or gratitude, but she knew her stepfather understood how grateful she was.

Her earliest memory was of Arthur Fitzroy eating up her carrots so her mother would not scold her for leaving her vegetables. He had done so much for her, even given her his name; and she knew he had even put aside a dowry for her, something he was not legally required to do.

He was a good man. A good man like Stuart.

Arthur beamed. "It is settled then! Let us get these wonderful lords and ladies leaping! Now, I am going to find my wayward daughter—Selina, I am sure you can make all of the arrangements. How difficult can it be?"

Caroline laughed, and she laughed frequently over the next few days at her naïve father's attempts to get everything prepared in time.

It was not as simple as her Papa had thought to organize an engagement ball at the drop of a hat, despite the number of times his wife gently reminded him.

Invitations had to be sent, food and wine ordered, and Caroline was given the good fortune of being able to choose not one, but two new gowns from their dressmaker for such a prestigious occasion.

"So I can decide on the night which is my favorite," she explained to her bemused Papa.

The snow that had threatened did indeed come the very evening Caroline and Stuart's engagement was announced, thick and heavy. Just as it did every year, it reduced London to a slow meander rather than the typical canter.

Nothing could be organized with speed, no matter how the Fitzroys may wish it, so it was in fact a good few weeks before everything was ready.

When that morning finally arose, Caroline woke with a feeling of anticipation.

CHAPTER THREE

THIS WAS THE moment: the first time she and Stuart would appear in Society formally as the future Dr. and Mrs. Walsingham. The hair on the back of her neck rose every time she thought about it.

Only a few more hours. A few more hours, and she would be on Stuart's arm for the world to see.

As carriages started to draw up outside, Caroline tried to find her missing glove in the bedchamber she shared with Jemima.

"I know it's here somewhere—there is absolutely nowhere else it could—"

"You're an engaged woman." Jemima's voice had no harshness in it, just surprise, as though it had only just dawned on her.

Caroline straightened her back and looked at her stepsister. Perhaps if they had met differently, had not been forced to grow up under the same roof, they could have been friends. Now it was almost too late.

"I know," she said finally. "Isn't it strange?"

Lifting her eyes to meet Jemima's, Caroline was surprised to see there was genuine emotion within them.

Jemima opened her mouth to speak, hesitated, but then continued. "You've always just been... Caroline. And now you are going to be living elsewhere, and," and here she swallowed, "and be Mrs. Walsingham."

A smile blossomed across Caroline's face. Mrs. Walsingham. What a marvelous thought. she would have to start to practice her new name. "Yes, I…"

Her voice trailed away. Jemima's eyes had drifted into vagueness, as though she had completely forgotten her sister was there.

"Jemima!"

Her stepsister jumped and turned, wide eyed.

"Jemima, what on earth has got into your head that you should be so far away?"

"Nothing of consequence."

Jemima's answer was brief and curt, which was most unlike her. She normally leapt at the chance to tease her sisters or bemoan their choices. At the very least, a conversation could not be considered complete unless Jemima had contributed.

What was wrong with her?

And then it hit her. Caroline suddenly recognized the symptoms her stepsister was displaying; she had experienced them herself when she had first met Stuart.

The signs of love.

A knowing smile appeared on her lips, and she moved to her bed, sitting on it to face the window. "You've been quiet, Jemima."

"Quiet?"

"*Too* quiet," Caroline said, noticing the worried tone in her stepsister's voice. "This is not like you. Normally you would have snapped at me—or shouted at me—or told me how irksome it was for you, having me talk about Stuart…Dr. Walsingham…continuously. Yet you have not crossed me with a single harsh word all morning!"

What was Jemima thinking? She was such an inscrutable character.

"It's nothing. Leave it, Caroline."

"But—" Caroline was intending to say much more, but the bedchamber door opened and her mother walked in, bustling toward her with a glove in her hand.

"Caroline Fitzroy, if you do not have things nailed down around you, they start to walk away. Here, I found this."

"Thank you," she said gratefully, snatching the long cream glove from her mother's hands. "I was about to tell you. I do not believe Jemima is entirely well. She has not been herself for the last day or two, and in the last hour, she has behaved in a most peculiar manner."

"I am quite well, I assure you," was Jemima's lackluster response.

"Unwell! You certainly do sound out of sorts, Jemima. Have you eaten anything which you believe may have disagreed with you?" After taking a few steps forward, she continued, "You do not look sickly."

"I am one and twenty years old, not a child!" Jemima protested as the older woman pressed her hand against the younger's forehead.

"You are a little warm," continued Caroline's Mama, ignoring the outburst. "But nothing of any consequence, nothing that would concern me enough to fetch a doctor—unless you wish me to, Jemima?"

Caroline looked at her stepsister, expecting her to smile. They all teased each other in the Fitzroy household, and it was a joy to finally include Jemima in that—but instead all Jemima said was, "I am quite well."

And so Caroline grinned. "Perhaps Mama, Jemima *is* sick, but we do not know the exact cause yet—but will tonight!"

Whatever effect Caroline was hoping her words would have on Jemima, she certainly received a reaction. Both her mother and Jemima turned to stare.

"Tonight?" Her Mama appeared just as confused as she had been before. "What is happening tonight?"

Caroline could not stifle her giggle. "Perhaps Jemima is *love-sick*. Perhaps her cure will be attending my engagement ball this very evening!" Her giggles increased. "Who is he, your young man follower? Butcher, baker, or candlestick maker?"

"Now, now then," said her mother reprovingly, "there is no reason to tease your sister."

"There is plenty of reason to tease my sister!"

Caroline beamed. Why, this was wonderful. If her marriage to Stuart could affect a change, a softening between the Fitzroy sisters, was that not a second wonder?

Jemima finally spoke, moving to the console table where her and Caroline's jewelry for the evening had been laid out. "No one. There is no one that—"

But Caroline, who was usually the butt of Sophia's jokes, was rather enjoying herself. "Tinker, tailor, solider, sailor, rich man, poor man, beggar man, thief?"

"Interesting you should say that, my dear," said her Mama with a thoughtful look at Jemima. "Your Papa did mention inviting a young man of Jemima's acquaintance. A soldier, was he not?"

After almost twenty years, Caroline should have known by now, should have seen the warning signs.

As it was…

"What business is it of yours?" Jemima glared. "Are you so desperate to marry me off, to get rid of me that you would force me toward any gentleman I happen to converse with? I refuse to marry just to please you, and if that means that I end up an old spinster with no one to love me or care for me, then so be it!"

Caroline had no opportunity to explain the joke before her stepsister had stomped out of their bedchamber. They could hear her heavy footsteps all the way down the stairs.

She bit her lip. *Darn it—she had not intended to cause such upset.* It had all been a jest.

"Ignore her," said her mother with a sigh. "I am learning to. Come down when you are ready, dear."

Caroline sighed, pulled on the glove, and a smile crept across her lips as she thought of the ball downstairs. All she needed to do was spend the night in the arms of the man she loved.

"Again!"

"No!" Caroline laughed at the excited look on Stuart's face, several hours later.

It was as though they were completely alone, not surrounded by hundreds of people at the engagement ball, which many were saying had never been bettered.

"I simply cannot dance one more dance, my feet are in agony!"

"We have barely begun!" Stuart's smile made Caroline's stomach twist happily. How was it possible to love someone so much? "Some of these lords have been leaping since the musicians first struck up, and I have no wish to be seen as wanting! I am determined to dance every dance at my own engagement ball, and there is no one I would rather dance them with!"

The ballroom was filled with Society's most significant and admired personalities, as well as countless friends and family of the happy couple. Even the all-important paragon, Lady Romeril, had accepted their invitation.

The candles were burning, food was disappearing at a rapid rate, musicians were playing happily, and everyone had admired the splendid punch. Though the hours drew on, there were plenty of people lining up for the next set.

The ball was a triumph.

Caroline smiled at the man she adored. "One more dance, my love, then you must allow me to rest or I shall be exhausted!"

Stuart didn't, taking her hand, he led her toward the musicians as people around them applauded gently.

Pulled along behind him, Caroline caught a glimpse of his mother gesturing at them—but it was too late for whatever it was she wanted to discuss. The music struck up, and Caroline beamed.

And after all that agonizing over which gown to wear. She should have known immediately that the cream satin gown with the extra decoration was the right decision.

She was not…well, she did not believe herself to be proud. Yet it was pleasant to have the eyes of the world on her, hear their flattering remarks about her beauty, her gown, her ball, her impending marriage…

She had never felt more beautiful. To think she would spend the rest of her life with Stuart, end each evening with him, wake up every morning—and her face flushed—with him.

"Who is that?" Stuart asked her when they next came together in the row.

Caroline laughed as the dance continued. "There are more people here than I can count, Stuart—who are you talking about?"

A single finger pointed behind her and slightly to her left. "There. That man, talking with your sister."

As Caroline was spun around, she stared in the direction Stuart pointed and was amazed to see Jemima dressed in an elegant satin gown, standing by a man in uniform. A soldier. Surely not the soldier Mama had mentioned?

It did not look as if their talk was going too well.

"Arguing, rather than talking I think," Caroline muttered to Stuart when she was close enough to speak without being overheard. "What on earth is he doing here—and how does he know Jemima?"

Stuart chuckled. "There's obviously more to Jemima than meets the eye!"

"Drat," said Caroline, "and Esther not here to witness it! I hope she's finding Bath a pleasant enough place. She and Lucy alike have certainly missed out on a good deal of excitement!"

At this point the dance became so complex they were unable to continue their conversation—at least in speech. Each look they gave each other spoke of the way they felt. Each time their eyes met, she could feel their ardor fizzing in the few inches between them.

Caroline reveled in the first time they had been truly free to express how they felt about each other in public.

Never again would they have to hide their strong attachment for each other. Though Caroline blushed to think about it, she knew they would continue to attempt to meet alone, and enjoy each other's company, without fear of interruption.

Something tugged at her lower belly, and a warm flush rushed through her body. Stuart's smile deepened, as if he knew exactly what she was thinking, and when he came toward her once more, his hand reached a little lower than her waist.

"I would not be anywhere else in the world," he whispered in her ear, "except perhaps your bed."

Caroline's lips parted in unconscious pleasure, but they had no chance to continue their conversation. The musicians finished with a flourish, and the couples dancing bowed or curtseyed before applauding them.

She clapped politely along with them until her hand was taken by Stuart.

"Now, I know I promised to dance every dance with you," he began quietly.

Caroline laughed, tingles rushing up her spine at the merest contact with him. "Are you attempting to tell me there is another person here you would prefer to dance with? Is our engagement ball truly the suitable time to—"

Stuart chuckled and brought her even closer. "I was more thinking that every single person in this house will be here, enjoying the ball."

Caroline was expecting him to continue but he had stopped, fixing her with passionate eyes. "And?"

"And," whispered Stuart, "there will be no one wandering around the rest of the house. Why don't we go exploring," his hand brushing against her bosom as he gently moved to hold her waist, "and see what we can find?"

IT WAS A scandalous thing for Stuart to suggest, he knew, but by God a man was only human.

And look at her. The most beautiful woman in the world. The most tantalizing. The only one he wished to see naked and begging for release beneath him.

Stuart cleared his throat as he shifted his feet, waiting for Caroline's answer. If she didn't say yes quickly, he would have to hope no one saw the hardness lengthening in his breeches.

And she wanted to say yes, he could see it in her eyes. The dusky look of desire had clouded them, but there was no changing the blue of that sparkling gaze.

Something lurched painfully in his stomach. *By God, he wanted her.*

"Caroline," Stuart breathed.

She had no time to respond. A woman stormed past them, knocking into Caroline's shoulder with her carelessness.

It was Miss Jemima.

"Jemima? Who is your friend?" Caroline's head turned to follow her sister as she asked the question.

Stuart sighed. He had been so determined to find time alone with Caroline this evening, but each and every single moment he thought they could creep away, another person would come forward to congratulate them.

It was gratifying, of course. He was a lowly doctor from a country family, and the Fitzroys were one of the most well-connected families in London. The Earl of Marnmouth was even here.

But in many ways, Stuart thought with a sigh, *he wished they were completely alone, able to celebrate their impending marriage in their own way.*

Without so many well-wishers.

But he blinked. He was alone. Caroline had gone.

Jemima was standing in the set opposite the soldier with whom she had been arguing fiercely not five minutes before. Others were moving to create a new set. Stuart saw an elderly gentleman move forward with his mother, and Miss Arabella, her fiery hair piled high, had taken the hand of a young man he did not recognize. And there on the other side of Jemima, clearly waiting for him, was…Caroline.

Stuart sighed. They would be dancing again, then. Not that he would complain, he loved to leap about the place. But compared to what rhythm he and Caroline could have been enjoying in private…

He strode forward and soon reached the set. Standing opposite Caroline, he turned to look at the soldier. It was only then that he noticed the man, probably only a few years older than himself, was holding tightly to a crutch.

Stuart was about to introduce himself, but another couple joined on his other side and he was forced to agree with the gentleman who shook his hand most profusely that yes, he was a very fortunate man, and yes, it was a wonderful ball, and no, they had not chosen a wedding date as yet.

By the time he had extricated himself from the pitter patter of polite conversation, he saw there were now ten couples in the set, many of them lords, and a few dukes to boot. The Fitzroys were certainly well connected.

"Stuart—"

Caroline started to speak, but the music started in full force and she was obliged to leave off.

It was not a particularly complicated dance, nor a fast one, but within it the ladies began. It did not take long for the gentlemen and lords to leap into action alongside their partners.

Each and every time he came close to the gloriously beautiful woman who was to be his bride, Stuart found it more difficult to control his physical response to her.

His longing to have her in his arms, preferably alone and in bed, was building. Each time they moved toward each other, it was all Stuart could do to prevent himself from clasping his hands on her bottom, rather than her waist.

But thankfully the dance was almost over, and he had not lost his head yet. It was almost midnight, and by one o'clock in the morning the ball would come to a close. Then, perhaps, he could snatch some secret moments with—

His thoughts were sharply interrupted by a scream.

Stuart looked up. He knew that scream. It was his mother: she was staring terrified at the elderly man with whom she had been dancing. He was not following the pattern of the dance but was instead clutching at his heart, staggering, trying to stand with legs buckling underneath him.

The solider was between him and Stuart, and the man immediately moved to try to support the elderly gentleman—but both men fell. Screams rang out now from all around the room, and a huge rush of people moved forward. In a few short moments the elderly man was hidden by the crowd.

Stuart's training kicked in. Everything he had learned, every day he had studied, every hour he had worked came together.

"Make way, I'm a doctor!"

Stuart had to bellow to be heard, but the natural respect for the medical profession meant enough people stood aside to leave a clear path for him to the elderly man no longer moving on the floor.

Stuart barely thought about what he was doing, it was so automatic. He loosened the cravat around the gentleman's neck and sought a pulse at his wrist. He closed his eyes to concentrate, willing his fingers to find the beat, willing the man to live.

He waited and waited. There was nothing. The skin beneath his was already cooling.

Dropping the wrist to the floor, Stuart rose from his knees and looked out at the faces staring, some in confusion, some in horror.

"He is gone." Stuart tried to keep a neutral tone in his voice, but it was impossible to contain the response.

Screams pierced the air as his mother pushed toward him.

"Stuart!" Her face was ashen as Mabel Walsingham repeated his name in haste. "Stuart, I was to introduce you to him—that gentleman is…was, your Great Uncle Edward."

It was as though time had stopped. Stuart stared, his mouth

open, mind racing.

"It…it can't be," Stuart said thickly, emotion welling in his throat. "Great Uncle Edward lives abroad—he argued with Father, he did not want to know us—we never heard from him!"

"Who do you think paid for your university tuition?" His mother spoke quietly and quickly as a hubbub erupted around them. "Who do you think was your mysterious patron? He had come today to make peace, to reveal himself as our benefactor—and now he is dead!"

Stuart sank to his knees and cradled the elderly man's head in his lap.

"Great Uncle Edward?" It was more a question than a statement, but one look from his mother told him it was true.

"Uncle Edward," repeated Stuart in wonder, looking down at the man who had changed his family's life. His medical fees, after all, supported his mother and sister—and without the money for the training, he would not have been able to afford to complete his studies. He would have no profession, would never have come to London—would never have met Caroline. "Uncle Edward…"

Somewhere far off he felt a hand on his arm. He stared. It was wearing a large diamond ring on its fourth finger.

"You cannot help him now," said Caroline's voice softly. "You know that, Stuart."

"Come, Stuart."

Stuart found himself pulled to his feet as his mother spoke. There was a steely look in her eyes he did not recognize.

"Come," his mother repeated as she pulled Stuart along with her.

Caroline's hand slipped into his, and Stuart relaxed knowing she was there, knowing she was close.

That was what he needed now, the reassurance of the woman who mattered to him the most.

But his mother stopped and looked at the pair of them. Stuart could not tell exactly what was on her mind, but she looked at them almost pityingly.

"I am sorry, Miss Fitzroy, but I must speak to my son alone."

She turned and pulled her son away—and Caroline was left alone, screams and crying filling the ballroom as Stuart walked away.

CHAPTER FOUR

CAROLINE DID NOT know why, but she always felt safe in the library. There was something peaceful about the way the room was always quiet, the fire almost always ablaze, throwing a warmth and glow around the room.

Which was what made this fear still nestled in her heart so surprising.

This was the first time the leather and parchment smell of the books, the fire, and the comfort of the armchair had not calmed her nerves.

She could not see much out of the window from where she sat, but the dim street light opposite showed light snow was falling once again on London.

The gilt gold clock in the center of the mantelpiece chimed once more. *Three o'clock*, Caroline thought to herself wearily. Three o'clock in the morning, and still she waited for Stuart to appear.

It had always been their custom, if one of them became trapped in a conversation with one of her family, to meet in the library. The door was close to the hall, so she was sure if Stuart had done the unthinkable and gone home, exhausted, she would have heard the door.

Most of the guests had left shortly after the elderly gentleman had collapsed. No one had wished to stay, and she could hardly blame them.

It was fortunate, Caroline thought drily, she did not depend on the good opinion of Society for her confidence, for she was sure her engagement ball would go down in legend as the one which killed a guest.

Her cream gown was scuffed at the hem after so much dancing, her corset tied uncomfortably tight after wearing it so many hours. Caroline shuffled uncomfortably, wondering whether it would be socially acceptable to loosen the ties of her gown at the sides—but then, Stuart could come in at any moment. She would have to wait a little longer before she could release herself.

Another yawn threatened to close her eyes, but Caroline fought it just as she had all the others. She was determined to stay awake.

Her eyes glanced over to the door as it opened, and she rose along with her heart to greet him—but her mother's head peeped around the door.

"Still awake?"

Caroline smiled wearily. "I will wait a few more minutes. I am sure they will not be much longer."

Her Mama frowned reprovingly. "To be so long worries me. What more could they have to say to each other?"

"Are they still in the study?"

Her mother nodded. "I even think I heard her bolt the door—not something we have had to do for many years, not since you girls were tiny babes."

Caroline shrugged. "I am sure whatever it is they are discussing is very important, and I am just as sure that as soon as they are finished, we shall all be acquainted with it."

To Caroline's eye, her mother did not look so sure, but the look passed in a moment.

"I am sure you are right, my dear. I am to bed."

"Goodnight, Mama," Caroline said softly.

Her mother took one more concerned look at her and then retreated, closing the library door softly behind her.

Caroline sighed and rubbed at her tired eyes. Quarter past the hour rang out from the gilt clock.

"One more hour," Caroline murmured to herself under her breath. "I will stay awake for one more hour, and if he has not returned by then…"

Her voice trailed off. *What would she do if Stuart had not finished speaking with his mother by a quarter past four?* She had never stayed up all through the night before, and with all the dancing she had indulged in, she was not sure whether she would be able to even if she wished it.

It was not, however, something she had to worry about for long. The clock had not chimed the half hour when the library door opened once more and an exhausted looking man with an untied cravat and a weary expression stood in the doorway.

"Stuart!"

Caroline rushed to him, flinging her arms around him. He seemed wooden, as though he had forgotten how to embrace another.

"Stuart?" Drawing back, Caroline was shocked to see Stuart was pale. The natural laughter ever present in his expression was gone. "Stuart, I am so sorry about the elderly gentleman—he was a relative, was he not? What have you discussed with your mother?"

As if he were an automaton, Stuart raised his arms to disentangle her own from around his neck, and stepped around her into the library. Caroline turned on her heels to stare at him as he fell into the armchair she had just vacated.

"You will never," he said heavily in a tired voice, "believe what I have just heard."

Tiny daggers scratched away at Caroline's heart. Closing the door to give them some privacy, she strode across the room and fell into the armchair opposite Stuart's. She reached for his hands. They were cold.

"Stuart, what on earth did your mother say to you?" Her voice was steady, although Caroline was surprised she had managed it.

What had frightened or shocked a man so steady and calm as Stuart? A doctor, after all, whom she had always considered utterly unflappable?

Worse, had Mrs. Walsingham managed to convince, finally, her son to abandon her? Caroline's heart contracted painfully. Was it possible at their engagement ball?

"To think," said Stuart slowly, pulling his hands from hers, "she had tried to tell me—and even in her letter to me, you recall I told you, she mentioned some important news. Yet even I could not have supposed something like this."

Stuart pulled away his cravat and started to tangle it in his hands. Caroline caught a glimpse of the top curls of his chest. Normally that sight would be leading her down a path of unimaginable pleasure, but she could not feel further from that now. His coat had been removed and discarded, she knew not where, and even his waistcoat was hanging open.

Closing his eyes, Stuart dropped his head into his hands.

"You are frightening me now," Caroline said, concern trickling into her voice. "In God's name, Stuart, tell me!"

Stuart let out a huge sigh, then said in a dull voice, "My Great Uncle Edward was not my Great Uncle Edward."

Caroline felt nothing but confusion. *Not his great uncle?* "That doesn't make any sense."

The more she examined him, the more her concern grew. It was shocking, yes, to see any person die. It had been the first time she had seen anything so startling, and would undoubtedly dream about it for weeks.

But Stuart was a medical man, a professional. *Surely he should not be so overwhelmed?*

The gentleman had been family, yes, but a distant relation from what Caroline could make out, a man Stuart had never met before today.

Stuart raised his head. "I suppose what I should really say, in all accuracy, is that my Great Uncle Edward was not *only* my

Great Uncle Edward."

"I don't understand," Caroline said, hands folded in the lap of her cream satin gown.

She waited as Stuart sat motionless, as though he was collecting the words from his mind and attempting to put them in the right order. Finally, he looked up and met her eyes.

"My Great Uncle Edward," said Stuart flatly, "was the fourteenth Earl of Cheshire."

Caroline stared, blinked twice, then shook her head slightly.

My Great Uncle Edward was the fourteenth Earl of Cheshire.

The words rang in Caroline's mind. They did not make sense. He was delirious with exhaustion, that was it.

"No. No, he wasn't."

"Yes," Stuart said heavily.

"No," Caroline repeated, shaking her head. She had to make him understand, the poor man was exhausted. What on earth had his mother been saying to confuse him so? "The fourteenth Earl of Cheshire is Frederick Montgomery, and he lives abroad."

He was a famous man, albeit he had spent little time in England. The recluse earl, the earl who had vowed never to return to British shores.

He had been a figure of some fascination in the Fitzroy household when Esther had announced last year that she would marry him and become a countess. It was only when their mother pointed out that he was grown, and undoubtedly married himself, that her sister abandoned hopes of a title.

Stuart smiled gently. "So thought I—so thought we all. But Frederick Edward Montgomery had a sister, Agatha, and she… she had a daughter called Mabel. She married and became Mabel Walsingham."

Caroline's mouth fell open. "You…you are in earnest."

She fell back into the armchair, attempting to comprehend what had just been said. So, a family relation of Stuart's had a noble title—it was a surprise, considering the poverty Stuart had managed to lift his mother and sister from, thanks to his hard work and diligence.

"Trust me, I did not believe it myself at first," Stuart's voice had regained a little more of the buoyancy she knew so well. "But I had always known my father and Great Uncle Edward had fallen out some years ago. I know now that was because the fourteen Earl of Cheshire did not approve of his favorite niece marrying a country doctor. My father."

"But," and here Caroline laughed, unable to take it all in. "This is surely impossible—surely your mother would have told you!"

Stuart shrugged. "Why should she? He and my father argued bitterly the year before my father died, and Great Uncle Edward never left Italy nor returned to England after that. We had never met him, he never communicated with us, he had disavowed all children of my father—why should she trouble herself with him?"

Caroline let out a long breath, but none of the tension building in her shoulders released. "Well, I have to admit that I am relieved. I was sure your mother had something of great import to tell you, dragging you away from me like that! I am glad it is nothing serious."

But as she smiled, Stuart did not.

"There is more." His voice was heavy.

Caroline winced at the timbre of his voice. "More?"

He leaned forward, took both of her hands in his, and looked deeply into her eyes. "My Great Uncle Edward, who was the fourteenth Earl of Cheshire, had one sister. That sister had two daughters, my mother and her sister. My aunt never married."

It was as though he was trying to tell her something through the power of his eyes, but Caroline had no idea why his family tree should be of any interest to her.

Had he not complained, just last week, at the complexity of the family trees of others?

"I know there is probably something very important in what you have just said," she said helplessly. "But it is past half past three in the morning, Stuart, and I cannot understand what you are trying to tell me."

Stuart tightened his grip on her hands and spoke slowly in a low voice. "I am the fifteenth Earl of Cheshire."

It was as though the entire world stopping moving. Its orbit around the sun was brought to a sudden stop, and everything was deadly still and quiet.

The words Stuart had spoken rang out in the room, echoing off the books surrounding them, echoing in her ears. The more she heard them, the less they made sense.

"No, you can't be." Caroline shook her head as she spoke. "You're Stuart—my Stuart. You're Dr. Stuart Walsingham."

"Plain Dr. Stuart Walsingham no longer," Stuart said quietly, relaxing his grip on her hands, as though realizing he was clenching them too tight. "I am now Dr. Stuart Walsingham, the fifteenth Earl of Cheshire."

The words could not sink in, and Caroline laughed, her nerves overwhelming her.

Stuart...an earl?

"You cannot be serious! Stuart, this is something that happens to other people, it does not happen to us!" Caroline could not help the words spilling from her mouth. "We do not inherit earldoms, or diamond necklaces—we are the people that invite people to engagement balls and get married in the spring, and hear about other people inheriting earldoms!"

Stuart leaned back in his chair. "I do not know what to tell you," he said quietly. "That is who I am now."

Her eyes took in his exhausted expression, the loose shirt—and then something clunked into her mind with such force, Caroline was surprised she was not knocked to the floor.

"So," she said quietly, heart thundering, "are you telling me I am currently engaged to be married to the fifteen Earl of Cheshire?"

A deep sigh and shrug was all Stuart's reply.

Caroline could not help but laugh. "This is ridiculous—you are an earl! And I am just... well, I am just a gentleman's daughter! Earls do not marry people like me. They don't dance with people like me—they rarely speak to people like me!"

Stuart said nothing. His gaze had drifted off into the distance.

Caroline pondered for a moment. *Stuart was an earl. An earl! A title.* It was wild, it was ridiculous—and it had actually happened!

Then a thought struck her. "Does that mean you will have to give up medicine?"

"I do not rightly know," Stuart confessed. Heavy lids looked exhausted as lines gathered across his forehead. "I have never heard of anyone within the nobility working for a living. It is not something I have ever given much thought to, but no names come to mind."

"But you love your work," said Caroline softly, reaching out an arm to stoke the fire with the poker. Sparks flew up, the flames casting Stuart's face into heavy shadow. "Would not you be sad to leave your patients?"

Stuart nodded. "I have worked so hard to get where I am, yet now I have climbed higher than ever without any action of my own. I will admit it is a strange and unsettling feeling."

"I will have to learn better manners quite quickly," said Caroline with a smile, heart beating nervously despite her show of confidence. "Now we are going to be mixing with the very height of Society!"

That was enough to break the stern look on Stuart's face. "You will require no such thing! You know that you match—nay, exceed every expectation I have of you! I sit down and tell you that our whole lives are going to be turned upside down, and for the foreseeable future, I tell you that you are going to be a countess—"

"A countess!" *Dear God.* Her mind had not reached that logical step yet.

"Yes, a countess," said Stuart emphatically, "and we shall not be able to live in London, at least not all year round. We will see much less of our friends and family."

"Stuart, this changes everything."

He nodded darkly. "This does indeed change everything. Who could have ever supposed that ten lords leaping would change our lives so irrevocably?"

CHAPTER FIVE

CAROLINE DID NOT sleep that night. It was past seven o'clock in the morning when she let Stuart out by the side door into the brisk morning air, and she could already hear her parents in the breakfast room.

She sighed, eyes itching, shoulders tight, feet aching, heart weary.

Words mingled in her memory with painful thoughts, questions neither she nor Stuart could answer…

What did this mean for their wedding? Their marriage? Their home, the life they had intended to live?

It had been a long night. It was to be an even longer few days, if she were any judge.

How long she could keep this news from her family, she did not know.

As she slipped upstairs to the bedchamber she shared with Jemima, Caroline splashed water onto her face to revive her. A cursory glance told her water was not going to be sufficient to hide the redness around her eyes.

Caroline stared at her reflection in the looking glass. It seemed almost madness that she was still wearing her cream satin engagement ball gown. It felt so long ago, like a dream. But she could not keep wearing it. She needed to change, and there was but one gown that would be appropriate.

Perhaps a little rest would help. Jemima was asleep in her bed, and as Caroline slipped into her own, she was sure the soft linen sheets would give her a few hours of rest.

She was wrong. She just lay there, staring up at the ceiling she knew so well, wondering what was going to happen next. What further revelations would be unveiled to her? She had only briefly spoken to an earl before, and had only seen the Duke of Axwick from a distance.

What did an earl look like? Sound like, speak like? Worse, how was she supposed to be a countess when she had no idea what one did all day?

She rose just past eleven. Her sisters were awake, too. That meant their breakfast, a late affair as was typical after a ball, was about to start.

Caroline crept out of her bed and left Jemima exactly where she had found her.

Opening the door to the breakfast room, she saw her parents seated at opposite ends of the table, with Sophia and Arabella on one side. Her Mama and Papa had evidently lingered in the room to hear the tales of the evening before.

Caroline took her place beside her mother and saw immediately concerned looks exchanged between her two younger sisters.

Well, that was to be expected. She was, after all, wearing her mourning wear.

"How did you sleep, my dear?" her Papa asked quietly.

Caroline stretched out her shoulders. "I did not, Papa."

"Not at all?" Sophia was all wide-eyed surprise. Having not attended the engagement ball until the early hours, she was the only member of the family who seemed truly awake. "Why on earth not, Caroline—did the ball go on so long?"

"A gentleman was…was taken ill last night," said Arabella softly, casting a worried look at their father, her hair loose and falling down her shoulders. "Many of us were very concerned about him. I am sure Caroline could not sleep for worrying about him."

A clatter on the stairs told the family that Jemima was up, and sure enough she stepped into the room and sat between Caroline and her father.

"Well, we will not have to worry about him falling ill again," said her Papa with a sigh.

Every pair of eyes turned to him.

"And he's really gone? Truly?"

Caroline could hear the disbelief in her mother's voice, but one look at her father was enough to tell her that all her sisters had been waiting for this moment.

"Yes."

"No!" Arabella stared in shock. Sometimes Caroline forgot the three years age difference between them. Eighteen felt a long way away. "I cannot believe he died at your engagement ball!"

"Well, it is true," said Caroline curtly, reaching out for the dried ham before her, placing a huge amount she knew she would never be able to eat onto her plate. "And the gentleman in question was Stuart's—Dr. Walsingham's Great Uncle Edward. And Stuart—Dr. Walsingham, that is, is in complete shock."

There was silence except for the scrape of butter on bread.

That was all she could say. Caroline could not bear to speak the words which would be all the more shocking to her family. Could not bear to be the one who told them of the drastic change in Stuart's circumstances.

In her own.

"What does that mean for you, Caroline?" Sophia's voice was soft, her eyes full of worried curiosity. "So unfortunate, too. Mrs. Walsingham never did like you."

What could she say to that? That she was about to become a countess? That her whole world was changing? That the friends of her childhood and family may no longer be able to visit her? That she would be forced to leave London, to live in a big, draughty old house in the country that no one had lived in for decades, and play lady of the manor?

But she had to say something. All her family were staring expectantly. They knew she had conversed late into the night with Stuart, they were awaiting something.

Yet it was not her place to reveal such things. So exhausted had she been by the end of their conversation, she had not thought to ask what she was permitted to reveal.

"It is complicated...the family tree is a complex one, and I am not entirely sure..." Caroline swallowed. Her mouth was dry. "I think there is little change, but Walsingham said...I do not think we should speak of the dead."

It was the only reply that Caroline felt strong enough to make, and her mother did not appear convinced but did not badger her and instead raised a hand to her head. She had evidently indulged a little too much last night. "Come now, darling. There must be more to it than that."

Caroline swallowed. She would not be drawn into this—not until she knew all the facts. Not until Stuart was here. He should be the one to tell her family.

Jemima was saying something to their father, but he brushed her off and said, "Was he unwell when he arrived?"

Caroline heard Jemima answer, but her response did not make any sense.

"No, Captain Rotherham was perfectly well when I last saw—"

"Not that we knew of," said Caroline's mother in answer to her husband's question. "But then, Dr. Walsingham had not seen his extended family for several years, he told me once at a card party."

Sophia was continuing to add more and more butter to her roll. "And he has no other relatives?"

Caroline shrugged. Her head ached, her eyes sore from staying up all night talking—arguing, really—with Stuart.

She could not accept that their lives were going to be that different, but it was as though Stuart knew something he had not told her. What on earth could change their lives even more?

What was there left to tell?

"It is most unfortunate," said Arabella, pouring herself more raspberry cordial, "that he should die at your engagement ball, Caroline—now that will be all anyone will remember, him leaping about and then not!"

Caroline glared at her sister, which was a rare occurrence. Could she not see how devastated she was?

Their Papa stepped in quickly. "Nonsense, a man that age could die at any time, any time at all! In fact, I am sure if he'd had the option of choosing the location of his demise, he would have chosen to be with his family, celebrating with them. As he was."

Silence fell upon the table, which was broken by a rather falsely cheerful voice.

"Well," said their Mama all too brightly, "I am sure poor Dr. Walsingham will have a lot on his plate now, what with helping his mother to organize everything. And a wedding, too, my goodness. Do you not think, Caroline?"

Caroline's left hand was holding a warm roll, only half eaten, and as she moved it around her plate, she saw the sparkle of daylight through the diamond ring on her finger.

Engaged to be married. Engaged to be married to a country doctor who had a roguish smile but would never do anything to hurt her. Engaged to a man who made her snort with laughter in a most undignified way.

Engaged to the Earl of Cheshire.

"I said," repeated her mother in a louder voice, "I am sure Dr. Walsingham will be very busy now, organizing his great uncle's estate now he is the only living family? Do not you think, Caroline?"

Caroline could feel the heat of everyone's gazes on her and could not look up. How could she face them, knowing their lives were about to irrevocably change?

"I have no wish to speak of this," she said finally.

Slipping from her chair, she left the room without looking at anyone, almost walking into the footman who was bringing in the post as she left.

There was no discourtesy, Caroline tried to convince herself. *I have an appointment to meet Stuart and his family today, and if I am going to make it there for midday as we agreed, I would have to begin my toilette now in any case. It will not take me long.*

It took, in actuality, far longer than Caroline had expected to prepare. One glance at herself in the looking glass showed her eyes were still painfully red, and it took several washes of her face to rid it of the pallor from yesterday's shocking events.

A death at one's engagement ball. Surely that did not bode well.

Taking up her most luxurious pelisse, as it looked to be inclement out, Caroline left the house before she had time to think.

That was what she wanted to do, keep on moving just a little faster than her body was comfortable with. As long as she kept moving, kept doing something, her mind would not be able to think about the thousand and one things whirling around her mind.

The snow which had fallen in the night while she and Stuart had spoken at length had settled, and in places had transformed to ice. Caroline saw at least one person slip. She concentrated on passersby to distract herself, which she barely managed.

Today was a slice of normality, luncheon with Stuart's family. That was all she had to concentrate on. Nothing out of the ordinary.

Making her way to the Strand was enough to keep her mind from thinking on any unsettling thoughts, and as she made her way to number 216, she saw Stuart, his mother Mabel, and his sister Victoria waiting for her outside the Twinings shop.

"I must apologize for my lateness," said Caroline almost out of breath by the time she reached them. "I will own I have not slept since we last saw each other!"

"Not slept at all?" Victoria took her arm under her own with her beaver fur shawl now covering them both. "You, my dear, are having far too much fun—what shall we do with you?"

Chattering away to her, Victoria strode into the tea shop with Stuart and Mrs. Walsingham following behind them. Victoria was Stuart's younger sister by only a year, and had shown no signs of courting any gentleman, Stuart had said, due to some sort of entanglement in her past.

Caroline had been expecting a letter from her daily, so jumped at the chance to question her while her mother was slightly out of earshot, their voices muffled by the beaver fur shawl.

Therefore, it was only when they had been seated by the obliging man in Twinings livery that Caroline noticed the strange expression on her future mother-in-law's face.

Stuart sat opposite her, with Victoria on her left and Mrs. Walsingham on her right. One quick look told her the news of yesterday was going to resurface before too long. Caroline's stomach lurched. She was not entirely sure she wished to discuss such a thing in public.

Mrs. Walsingham was one of those women who had not seemed to age in the last twenty years—and indeed, the only reason Caroline was able to remember she was a whole generation older was because her taste in clothes had not yet reached the nineteenth century.

Her gown had all of the frills and fancy decoration which had been so popular, and the waist line was far too low to be admired in today's popular Society.

Yet despite that, Caroline had tried to enjoy her company. She could conceive of no reason why Mrs. Walsingham should be glaring at her so viciously. *It must*, reasoned Caroline, *be something of the digestion that was ailing her.*

"Mrs. Walsingham," Caroline said gently. "Is there anything the matter?"

"Waiter!" Stuart interrupted, preventing his mother from replying. "Ah, good morning, sir. Yes, two pots of tea—one Early Grey, and one…"

"Lapsong, please," said Victoria, laying her gloves next to her and throwing a beaming smile at the young man who had a notepad and pencil in his hands.

Just like her brother Victoria had inherited the Walsingham charm, and her delicate features and beautiful chestnut brown hair meant the stuttering waiter was not the first man to fall victim.

"Lapsong it is, although how you can stomach the stuff is far beyond me," said Stuart, throwing a smile at his mother and Caroline. As far as Caroline could see, neither were convinced. There was a tightness around his eyes she did not like. "And a tray of sandwiches, and one of meats, and two of sweet cakes."

"Right you are, sir," said the poor young waiter, and with a nervous smile in the direction of Victoria, "madam."

He scuttled off as Victoria tried not to laugh. "Oh, young men are such darlings, aren't they Caroline? Although I do not believe Stuart has ever been quite that shy."

"I am not so sure," said Caroline, trying to match Victoria's buoyancy with her own, determined not to pay any attention to the grave look on Mrs. Walsingham's face. "The first occasion I ever met your brother, he was most arduously attempting to both play the pianoforte and catch my eye—and I must admit, he had little success with either!"

"Now, that is not true," said Stuart over Victoria's giggles. "I think I managed to finish off the concerto rather well, considering the fact there was an actual angel listening to me—or pretending not to listen behind a fan, having to nod politely to Mr. Cripwell!"

"And poor Miss Lucy!" Victoria said, her giggles showing no sign of subsiding. "It was one of her first entrances into Society, was it not? And she almost fainted with laughter, the poor soul!"

The conversation slowed as the first pot of tea and delicate china cups and saucers arrived, and Caroline had another chance to look at Mrs. Walsingham. She looked as pale as Caroline felt, but there was something else in her face. Sadness of some sort, or even a dark resolve.

Stuart coughed. "Shall I pour, Mother, or would you like to?"

Mrs. Walsingham did not answer. Instead, she turned to Caroline and said with a serious voice, "I assume Stuart has told you all that I told him last evening, after the untimely death of my Uncle Edward."

Caroline's stomach lurched, and her breath caught in her lungs. Was it customary to merely launch into such topics of conversation?

It did not seem as though Mrs. Walsingham had posed a question, so Caroline was unsure as to whether a reply was expected.

"What you two discussed afterward is private," Mrs. Walsingham said crisply, "and I would be wrong to ask you to repeat it. I assume the fact he will shortly be announced as the rightful heir—the *only* heir—to the Earldom of Cheshire was covered?"

"Mother," said Stuart quietly, as if he knew what his mother was going to say.

But Caroline smiled. She knew Mrs. Walsingham almost as long as she had known Stuart. There was nothing she could say which could truly unsettle her.

She was a little unusually formal today, it was true—but then such news would naturally make one formal.

"We did discuss it, yes," said Caroline, accepting the cup of tea Victoria, impatient as ever, had poured. "It was a shock, I admit, but it is starting to settle in me as time goes on."

"I hope you understand the change that is about to happen in my son's life," said Mrs. Walsingham, nodding to the waiter as he placed a large silver tray of exquisitely prepared sandwiches on the table. "I hope you understand the expectations which are now upon him."

Caroline almost sighed audibly with relief. This was about Stuart's occupation. Of course, he would need to decide whether to continue practicing medicine. "It will certainly be a difficult decision for him. Stuart has a passion I see every day—yet, I think you are right. I think he will eventually, and probably sooner rather than later, have to give it up."

Stuart almost dropped his cup of tea. He managed to retain a partial hold of it, but the clattering noise as it hit the saucer startled people around the tea room.

Caroline had not considered anything she had said in any way wild or rebellious, but her future mother-in-law was staring in complete shock.

"You…you agree, then," she said, a confused tone in her voice, "that Stuart should give it up?"

"Well, naturally," said Caroline, sipping her tea. It was still too hot to enjoy, so she placed it down and reached for a sandwich instead. "I mean, things can hardly go on exactly as they are."

"I am quite in agreement with you," Mrs. Walsingham spoke with quite obvious relief.

Caroline smiled, but was astonished to see both Victoria and Stuart were staring at her, astonishment on both of their faces—and sadness in Stuart's case.

"Caroline," he said, his voice wounded, "I cannot believe that you just said that."

Caroline blinked. *It was all very simple, wasn't it?* "Well, you know things cannot be exactly the same. You are the fifteenth Earl of Cheshire now! Whoever heard of an earl who was also a doctor?"

Understanding dawned on the two siblings' faces, but Mrs. Walsingham choked on her sandwich and had to take a large gulp of tea to clear her throat.

When she could speak, she stared at Caroline with an angry look. "A doctor? Do you think I was talking about Stuart giving up his medical practice?"

"Well, of course," Caroline said, confusion pulsing through her. "You said that there would be expectations of Stuart now."

"When you spoke of a passion that he would have to give up," said Mrs. Walsingham, speaking slowly and forcefully, "I assumed you were speaking of yourself!"

Caroline opened her mouth in horror. The room seemed to

slow, to darken around the edges. The clattering of teacups and murmur of conversation faded, leaving only the four of them in the center of the world.

Give him up...give up Stuart?

"I—Mrs. Walsingham, you cannot be in earnest!"

"Oh, she is," said Stuart darkly, reaching toward the plate and placing not one, not two, but four sandwiches on his plate.

"Give up me?" Caroline said, staring at Mrs. Walsingham, who returned her look defiantly. "Who in their right mind would suggest such a thing? I mean no offense, you know I do not, but why should our marriage plans be any different now Stuart is the fifteenth Earl of Cheshire?"

"Because he is above you!" Mrs. Walsingham said, and would undoubtedly have said more, but she was interrupted by her daughter.

"I still think that you are wrong about this, Mama!" Victoria was glaring at her mother. "Surely you would want a wife for your son who loved him no matter what title, if any, was alongside his name."

"I am sorry," said Mrs. Walsingham, her voice softening. "You know I like you, child—"

Caroline gaped. *How could she say that with a straight face!*

"—and I think you will make someone very happy as a wife, one day. But not my son. You are just a Fitzroy. What is a Fitzroy to the Braedons and Marnmouths and Devonshires of the world?"

Caroline could barely hear her, the ringing in her ears was growing louder and louder.

It was as though she was living in a nightmare, and she could not force herself to awaken.

The tearoom was spinning, heat rising through her body, making it impossible to think. Dizziness started to overwhelm her, but she fought it, desperate to continue the conversation.

"I-I love Stuart," she said desperately, "and I will marry none but him!"

Victoria sighed. "Mother, you know I think you are overreacting to this."

Caroline was grateful for her words but could not help but notice Stuart's silence. Why did he not speak? Why did he not defend her, state that he loved her, would marry her no matter what his mother said?

She caught his gaze. Stuart looked down at his plate.

"Then you tell me," Mrs. Walsingham said in a quiet voice, "exactly how you think we are going to pay my Uncle Edward's debts!"

Stuart looked up at these words. "Debts?"

Mrs. Walsingham sighed as though the weight of the world was on her shoulders. "He has been dead but twelve hours, and already the letters are starting to arrive. Yes, Stuart, debts. The earldom is mortgaged up to the hilt, and I see no other way to pay them than for you to find a girl just as nice as Caroline here, but more importantly, with money."

And that was the remark that pushed Caroline over the edge. "Just as *nice* as me?"

She rarely grew angry—it was one of the characteristics which so infuriated her sister Jemima—but this was too much.

The lack of sleep, her confusion, her grief and surprise as the death of a man at her engagement ball, the questions of her family, her love of Stuart—not to mention her red hair—all combined to create the perfect storm.

"I will have you know that you would be lucky, you hear me, lucky to find any other woman in this world as *nice* as me—and what's more, you would be hard pressed to find someone who adores your son as I do!" Caroline did not care that her voice had risen, that she was starting to elicit curious looks from around the tea room. The waiter who had been so taken with Victoria was blatantly gawping. "So, if you really want to try and blackmail your son into marrying a woman he does not love, and for all we know would not love him either, then you can try that, but I tell you now—you will not succeed!"

And with that, she stood up so violently her chair fell behind her, knocking into a couple seated behind them.

"I say!"

"Careful, miss!"

Ignoring their cries and the instinct to continue berating her future mother-in-law, Caroline stormed out of the tea shop.

CHAPTER SIX

C AROLINE DID NOT look where she was going. She did not need to know, she just needed to get as far away from the Strand, from that table, as possible.

Rage flowed through her veins. It was a new feeling, and like strong liquor, it consumed her, destroying her patience.

There was snow falling now, clumping over the snow and ice from the previous night. Trees wore dusty frock coats, and she passed several shops whose keepers were already pouring out, trying to prevent the snow from setting on their windowsills.

"Caroline!"

She paid little heed to those around her. Her blood was still boiling.

The very thought that Mrs. Walsingham could consider her unsuitable for her son, merely because she did not come with a big enough dowry—that was something which happened to other people, this sort of situation did not happen to people like her!

"The earldom is mortgaged up to the hilt, and I see no other way to pay them than for you to find a girl just as nice as Caroline here, but more importantly, with money."

This was madness, madness! Perhaps she would wake soon and it would be the morning of the engagement ball, and none of this had happened…

"Caroline, wait!"

How Jemima would crow, Caroline thought dully, *how she would gleefully reign over this misfortune of hers.* It was not enough that Stuart loved her, or that she loved him—no, there had to be a financial calculation before they wed, and sadly now the numbers just didn't add up.

"Will you not wait?"

A hand on her arm stopped her short, and she blinked. Looking around, Caroline realized she had no idea where in London she was. The hand on her arm was attached to a man, a man speaking as though he was a long way off.

"Caroline? Caroline, talk to me."

Caroline blinked. It was Stuart.

"You followed me," she said unnecessarily as she clutched at facts she both knew to be true and were not mortifying. "You followed me from the tea shop."

"Did you really think I was going to let you leave without speaking to you?" Stuart shivered in the cold December air. He had left his great coat behind in the tea room and snow was beginning to collect on his shoulders. "Did you really think I was going to let you go without a fight?"

"I…" Caroline tried to speak, but none of the sentences she tried to form made any sense.

How could she explain what that conversation had meant to her? How could she tell him just how mortifying it was to be measured, so publicly, and be found wanting?

"Do you really think," continued Stuart with a wry smile, "I was going to let you walk home in the snow without your pelisse?"

Caroline looked at him blankly, then at her pelisse in his arms, then back at Stuart. She did not have words to convey just how angry, how frustrated she was at that very moment.

She was not an angry woman. That was always Jemima. There was always so much excitement and drama around the eldest Fitzroy, Caroline had always attempted to be calm and gentle. To be the child who did not speak her mind at all times, who rarely voiced her opinions when they went against those of others.

It was only now she realized how damaging this had become. *When was the last time she had shouted, truly shouted?* When had she last defended herself? When had she ever rocked the boat to explain what she wanted, to show how she wanted to be happy?

"I know you have a right to be angry," said Stuart softly, "but we cannot talk properly here."

"Your mother never liked me," she shot at him. "Never!"

"I know," Stuart said, raising his hands as though trying to pacify an angry bull. "And—"

"This is madness!" she said helplessly. "One minute he's a lord leaping, and then he's dead—and you are a lord! An earl!"

"I know," repeated Stuart, "but this conversation must continue inside."

He looked around. Caroline saw they were starting to attract attention. A boot polisher and his customer were staring, and there was a rather uncomfortable look coming from a street urchin Caroline did not like.

"Well, we certainly cannot go to my home," she said sadly, blinking to prevent the tiny snowflakes crystallizing on her eyelashes, bitterness and irritation seeping into her words. "There will be too many questions…questions I do not currently know if I can answer."

"Then let us go to my rooms. My landlady will be out at this time, it will be quite safe." Stuart took her arm in his and began to walk slowly. Eventually Caroline's legs understood they were moving, and she fell into step beside him.

Not a word was spoken between them until they had reached his lodgings, entered through the back door, climbed the stairs, and finally stepped into his room and shut the door.

Stuart threw himself on his bed, shoes and all. Caroline just stood and let out a huge sigh, as if all of the frustration that she felt could be forced out by her lungs.

Oh, if only it were that simple…

"Now what do we do?" Stuart said darkly, staring at the ceiling.

"I do not know—it was your idea to come back here, to talk?" Caroline could not help but frame it as a question.

She had assumed—*wrongly, it appeared*—that Stuart had wished to say something to her in private, but he seemed to have little but dull acceptance.

"What is there to say?" Stuart spoke bitterly, not taking his eyes from the ceiling. "My mother has spoken."

"She is not your keeper, you are a grown man!" Caroline strode to the bed and sat on the opposite side to where Stuart was now lying. "You are bound by no promises to her, as you are to me!"

Stuart turned his head. "She is my *mother*, Caroline. No promises are required to the woman who gave me life! You truly think that I can just ignore all she says?"

"You truly think you can just leave me?" Her words were filled with horror and confusion, emotions she could no longer hide. "I hate to think it is that easy to walk away from me, but clearly I have to face that!"

Stuart's voice grew harder as he sat up. "I do not think you quite understand, Caroline—as the fifteenth Earl of Cheshire, I have responsibilities now!"

"Your responsibilities to me are of an earlier date," pointed out Caroline, desperate to keep the panic from her voice. She had to approach this as a rational, calm woman. Even if she did not feel it. "And I am still struggling to understand why they are so easy to ignore!"

Stuart rose from the bed. "It is just not about you now, Caroline! How many people do you think depend on the earldom for their home, their food, their occupations?"

Caroline stared as he began to pace around the room. "I do not know…a hundred, maybe more?"

"Try three thousand," said Stuart bitterly. "Above three thousand souls in this world depend on the lands on the earldom for their bread and butter, and if the earldom were to collapse, if it were sold off piecemeal to the highest bidder, who would protect them? Who would ensure their children would not go hungry, their grandparents would not go to the workhouse?"

Caroline stared. *This could not be happening.* "What about the countless people right here in London that depend on you every day?"

"No one here depends on me," he said dismissively.

"You think so?" said Caroline with a challenging air. "How many people do you see on your rounds each day? How many patients do you have on your books, several who could not afford the outrageous prices those quacks charge them for nothing more than kind words? How many lives have you saved since you came here, how many more would you save if you continued?"

"I can no longer be so singular in my thinking." Stuart halted his pacing and faced her at the end of the bed. "There are so many more people to think of and consider now, beyond yourself, beyond my own family. Every decision I make affects thousands! I would be a poor steward indeed if I did not stop to take stock when making such a decision as this."

Caroline rose from the bed and walked around it to face Stuart. *How could he speak of taking stock and making decisions, as though he were a callous landlord seeking rent?*

There was only one thing she could think to say, only one sentence that naturally slipped from her lips.

"But…I love you," she said simply.

THERE WAS NO guile in her tone.

Stuart groaned. He was unable to bear it all, this burden placed on his shoulders, a burden that had been his inheritance the moment he'd been born, though he had not known it.

With no time to prepare, no time to think, and a lifetime of responsibility ahead of him, there was nothing more that he wanted than to escape his predicament—and the perfect excuse for escape was right before him.

There Caroline stood. A physical emblem of his old life—a life which had disappeared not four and twenty hours ago. Sweet promise of a future now wrenched from him.

Stuart gave into the temptation and left behind all thought as he leaned forward and kissed Caroline full on the mouth, tasting her deeply as she wrapped her arms around him. Stuart almost groaned, such was the relief to touch her.

"I have wanted to do this," he said gruffly, wrenching his lips from hers for just one moment, "since you walked into our engagement ball. Oh God, Caroline!"

Caroline responded eagerly, seeming to pour all her frustrations into his willing arms and willing lips. Her hands wandered around his neck, pulling him closer. Stuart tried to maintain control, tried to keep the kiss chaste, but the hardness between his legs rubbing against her only stirred the fire within him, which had been building for days, weeks, months…

His hands moved, ripping off his waistcoat while still passionately kissing her, his tongue ravishing the warm softness, which Caroline opened willingly.

Before he knew it, instinct had entirely taken over. His hands were untying her gown. As the soft material peeled away, Stuart's fingers wandered over Caroline's skin, worshipping it, luxuriating in it, glorying in her.

She broke the kiss and looked deeply into Stuart's eyes. He could see the battle in her, the desire and yet the restraint.

"Caroline," he said raggedly, fingers fumbling at the buttons on his shirt, neck tie already thrown onto the floor, "I want you— and by God, I'm going to have you."

Strong hands threw down his shirt, and Caroline gasped at the sight of his chest. His mere physicality was enough to raise a response in her, he could see that, and their mutual passion raised a fire within him.

"Caroline…" he breathed.

Though hesitant, she obeyed the silent request he could not make. Gently at first, and then with more confidence, her fingers explored every inch of his chest. Stuart shivered as her fingertips brushed over him, as her mouth closed ardently on his lips once more. He could not help but groan at the sweet torture of having her so close, yet not close enough.

Nothing was close enough.

His hands encircled her, bringing her near, then wandered down toward her bottom.

Caroline seemed to understand, toes rising to bring her center toward the hardness that was making demands of Stuart, just like every time he and Caroline found themselves in this lustful position.

But this was different.

Caroline's eyes fluttered with desire, nothing holding her back. Stuart caught a glance of the large and exquisite diamond on her left hand, and his body twitched as he imagined laying her down on their marriage bed, stripping every single item of clothing from her, and making love to her, again and again, until they were beyond worn out…

"Caroline!" Stuart's eyes widened as the hands that had previously been exploring his chest moved lower—lower than they ever had before.

The lightest of touches was all she needed to make. Stuart moaned as her fingers caressed his manhood, straining to break free. Stars appeared in his vision, and he could feel his knees starting to buckle.

No wonder people longed to be married, Stuart thought wildly, *if this was a taste of the delights that awaited them.* If he didn't take her soon, he would burn up completely.

They were so in tune that Caroline did not need to be told; his yearnings clearly matched her own. Her gown was untied and just needed the slightest of tugs to pool to the floor, leaving Caroline in her undershift.

Stuart swallowed. They were dancing along a dangerous line

here, but they had danced before.

"You have never been so beautiful," he said unevenly, his voice catching in his throat, hands itching to remove that one last piece of clothing keeping him from his heart's desire.

Though she stood before Stuart in scant clothing, Caroline did not appear embarrassed. The situation did not feel…wrong. But quite the contrary, it felt natural, as though greater pleasures they could have ever experienced were soon to be had.

Stuart's left hand tenderly moved to her waist, and Caroline gasped at the contact now there was only one meager layer between his fingers and her. His other hand went straight for her breast. *Well,* Stuart thought wildly as he moaned at her softness, *how could he stop himself?*

Caroline arched into him as his rhythmic caress stoked the longing within her. Her breath shortened, and Stuart could feel her ardor in his very being as he lowered his lips to capture hers once more.

"I want this," Caroline said through the kiss, her hands once more traveling down to that sensitive part of him. "Stuart, I want you so—"

No words were necessary. Caroline tried desperately to kiss Stuart harder and harder—but this only caused his manhood to twitch, desperate to be free from his breeches. He growled and moved the hand that had been holding her steady at her waist to cup her pert bottom.

He attempted to take a steadying breath. This was where he should stop. This was where they had almost always stopped, save for that smattering of times that his fingers had teased her to ecstasy, like the one day when he had proposed.

They had to restrain themselves. They had to wait.

Wait for what? Stuart hardly knew what the future held now, it was so uncertain. The only real thing in the world, the only thing he was sure of, was that he wanted her.

"I love you," Caroline murmured.

And that was when he abandoned all attempt at control. As

he watched jolts of pleasure shoot through her body from that thumb giving so much bliss at her nipple, his other hand moved around to rest on her core.

Stuart sighed as he felt the sheer amount of heat coming from her. She was ready, she wanted this. *She wanted him.*

But before he released his fantasies and desires upon her, he was determined to give her more satisfaction than she could have ever imagined. He had to make sure she never regretted this moment.

In a swift movement, Stuart moved his hand underneath Caroline's shift, slipping a finger within her. Caroline jolted, then jolted again as the movement merely crushed his fingers deeper into her, causing ripples of delectable thrill to soar through her body.

"Oh, Stuart," she moaned, her hands gripping his neck tightly as pleasure made her legs shake.

Stuart had barely begun his work, but he did not pause. His mouth pressed hard against hers, his tongue taking and giving pleasure from her mouth whilst his other hand gloried in the heaviness and softness of her breast. His left hand began to move, slowly but sure, creating a rhythm that stirred her, rising the storm, throwing flames onto the fire.

He had to give her pleasure. He had to show her just how much she meant to him.

Caroline whimpered as he watched the pleasure start to consume her. Her legs were growing weak, Stuart could feel it in the grip around his shoulders, but he instinctively reacted, his hand leaving her breast and moving to her back to steady her.

"Stuart," Caroline whispered shakily, "I...I think I'm going to—"

And then she did: climax scattered across her body, and she threw her head back as her body spasmed, her shouts of joy muffled by his kiss.

Whether he would regret it later or not, he knew that there was only one thing that was going to satisfy him.

"Stuart, that was…" said Caroline, eyelashes fluttering as she leaned heavily on him. "I have never…that was—"

"Enough talking," said Stuart brusquely, his desire for her making it difficult to speak. "I know what I want from you, Caroline, and I know you want it, too. Stop me if you want to, but I hope to God you don't."

He looked into her eyes, saw the understanding there, and waited. She said nothing but leaned forward to kiss him.

In one swift movement, he had pulled her undershift off.

Caroline gasped, but her hands did not move to cover her nakedness. Instead, she stood, staring at Stuart as if willing him to touch her.

For a heart-stopping moment, Stuart did not feel as though he could.

He had seen so much of Caroline, it was true, but he could never have imagined such perfection in the human form outside of the statues that graced the streets of Rome. Her heavy breasts and the curved stomach that ran straight into the curls where his fingertips had teased, the gentle line of her collarbone threw her neck into elegant relief. Her legs, and here Stuart had to swallow, long and slender and perfectly formed for the full roundness of her hips.

She was perfection.

There was nothing that he would change, and his body responded to her in the only way it knew how.

"Caroline," he murmured as he quickly pulled off his boots and undid the tie of his breeches, allowing them to fall to the floor.

Caroline's eyes widened as she stared for the first time at the cause for the hardness she had so often felt.

She did not speak, merely moved. The feeling of her bare skin on his created a reaction in Stuart so strong that his resolve, hanging by a thread as it was, completely snapped.

They had been only inches from the bed, and with a simple push, Caroline fell backward onto it, Stuart unable to take his eyes from her. Before either of them could speak, he had covered her body with his own.

The wetness Stuart had felt between Caroline's legs was now starting to make it very difficult for him to think of anything else. As he kissed her, his hands moved to her bottom, clasping it forward and almost shouting at the joy of it all. Her hair had escaped from its pins and lay resplendent on his pillow, as if his world had been set alight.

Stuart was lying beside her, but Caroline's legs were closed, preventing him entrance. They were utterly naked, a line they had never crossed before.

"I'm ready," said Caroline, reading his mind, her voice uneven as she panted, shaking slightly as she parted her legs. "I love you, Stuart."

That was all he needed to push him over the edge. With a kiss just above her breasts that made her shudder, Stuart gently pushed her legs apart and pushed the tip of himself into her.

He had to close his eyes to retain control, and the little gasps she was starting to make was music to his ears.

But he mustn't rush. The thought of hurting her was abominable—he would not do it. He would be master of himself, even if it killed him.

It was about to kill him.

He could barely breathe, barely think, as his manhood slowly entered her, the wet tightness pushing him right to the edge.

"Oh, Stuart," murmured Caroline as she shuddered beneath him. "I want all of you, I want you now!"

He groaned, then gave her exactly what she requested. Burying himself to the hilt, he sank everything that he was into her warm wetness, causing him to bite his lip with the pleasure.

This was intimacy, this was the height of being with someone: when you could feel every twitch of theirs echoing inside you.

But this was not all. He kissed her, knowing new heights of pleasure were about to begin.

Bringing himself almost all the way out, Stuart rocked back into her, and Caroline juddered as he took them to another precipice of pleasure.

"Stuart?" she said uncertainly, and then, "Stuart!" as he began to build a rhythm, pushing himself into her again and again, causing wonderful friction that was building to a cliff top he was ready to jump over.

Stuart tried to calm his ragged breathing, determined to give her as much satisfaction as she was willing to take, hoping he would be able to hold off climaxing until then.

But he did not have to worry: it was as though Caroline was built for pleasure as she raised her hips, her eyes fluttering and her moans more than enough to make Stuart desperate for his own release.

But he would wait for hers first. He would not be a selfish lover; he had promised himself that the first time his errant fingers had brushed up against Caroline's breast and she had gasped.

He would make her shout his name again.

And then it came.

"Oh, Stuart!" Caroline screamed as her body thrust and jerked as her climax utterly consumed her.

His whole body shuddered with longing finally fulfilled.

And then there was silence. Stuart fell onto the bed beside her as Caroline's eyes fluttered, his mind trying to gain composure.

He rolled a few inches away from her and tried to catch his breath. It was several minutes before either of them spoke.

The realization of exactly where they were struck Stuart like a lightning bolt. That was it, then. They had crossed the line. They could never go back.

And he'd been a damned fool not to retrieve a French letter from his damned pocket.

"Stuart," Caroline whispered.

"Mmm?" was all the reply Stuart could manage as dread rushed through him.

"Stuart, what have we done?"

CHAPTER SEVEN

"**I** DO NOT quite understand," Caroline's Papa said, putting down his small cup of coffee, something he indulged in every morning. "You are telling me Dr. Walsingham—*your* Walsingham—has inherited an earldom?"

The looks of concern from both her parents did nothing to calm Caroline's nerves.

A constant stream of worry poured from them to her as soon as they heard the news, when there was already more than enough worry within her.

How could she and Stuart have been so rash yesterday? After months of calm—*well, relative calm*—they had made just one mistake. A mistake that could have a very real consequence, an unavoidable one, in just nine months.

Caroline swallowed. She had always thought women who were with child would always know they were. Was that why her stomach felt so conflicted, so nauseated? Surely, she would not know yet if she was with child.

This was not going to be the Christmas she had expected.

If only her mother had given more details than the vaguest understanding of how a child could be made. If only her fluttering hands across her stomach could tell…

"I do not know all of the details," Caroline said quietly, trying not to meet her sisters' eyes—not that Jemima would have noticed, she seemed unreasonably happy for some unknown reason, with curling papers left in her hair. "He is having to spend a little time with some lawyers to…to fully ascertain the details of his Great Uncle Edward's estate."

"Well, I am sure much will have to change in the wedding if you are truly to become a countess!" said her mother, picking up a peach from the bowl on the table. "It is not every day a wedding of this kind occurs, after all, and we shall certainly want a much larger trousseau for you now."

Caroline shuffled uncomfortably on her chair. She was wearing one of her older gowns, a cream one with sky blue edging, and it had always fitted her perfectly before. *Was it a little tighter?*

"It is true then?" Arabella's voice was delicate and soft. "He really is the new Earl of Cheshire."

Caroline nodded. The last thing she wanted to do was to discuss this with her family, because she knew eventually the other truth—that Mabel Walsingham was set against the marriage taking place—would eventually follow.

She was relieved Jemima was talking hurriedly with their father, for it meant her stepsister was not going to carry on about it all.

"You see, Papa, I wanted to ask you—"

"But an earldom!" Arabella's eyes were wide. "Caroline, that will mean you'll be—"

"Please," Caroline managed to say, breath tight in her lungs. *Oh, this was unbearable!* "Can we speak of something else. Anything else?"

"I must congratulate Mrs. Castle on finding these peaches, in December of all times!" her Mama said with a breathless smile. "She certainly works wonders."

"I just wish we could have oranges as well," piped up Sophia. "I do not see why we should have peaches all of the time!"

"Fie, Sophia," said Arabella with a slight smile. "Peaches all of the time? We have not had peaches in a good three weeks, and you know that they are Mama's favorites."

Any other day, any other time in her life, Caroline would have joined in the teasing of Sophia—it so rarely happened that all the Fitzroys tried to take advantage of it if they could.

Not today.

Now all she could hear was the cries of scorn Society would rain down on her if they saw her eight months hence, heavy with child.

What would her parents say if, and here Caroline swallowed hard, *they knew what she and Stuart had done?* Despite her indifference to the opinion of Society on her engagement ball—notorious death of a gentleman notwithstanding—she knew losing her reputation in such a way would mean she would immediately become an unsuitable bride for any man, let alone the Earl of Cheshire.

So, what was to be done? What could she do? Was she forced to wait to see whether or not she was with child? Was there any way of telling? Would she recognize that feeling?

Her mother smiled and replied to something Jemima had said, but Caroline had not quite caught. "No imposition whatsoever."

"But what is to be done?"

The words had escaped Caroline's lips before she realized she was still seated at breakfast with her family, and their concerned and confused looks proved they had no idea what she was talking about.

At least, not yet.

Though she had fought the emotions for what felt like forever, she no longer could prevent the fear, the frustration, the absolute terror Stuart was about to abandon her—and perhaps, their child.

Caroline burst into tears. What had been below the surface for hours flowed down her cheeks.

"Oh, my darling." Her Mama instantly slipped into mothering mode, rising from her chair to envelope her in a hug.

Caroline saw over her mother's shoulder that Jemima had

slipped from the table and left the room, and she was glad of it. She did not want to have this outburst thrown in her face in a later argument.

"I know it can be somewhat disconcerting," said her father kindly, "discovering something like this. But you will soon see, Caroline, that almost everything will return to normal."

Sophia stared at her oldest sister in wonder. "I have never seen you cry before, Caroline," she said uncertainly.

"Do not fret my dear," said their mother, pulling back from Caroline and drying her tears with her handkerchief. "It is all of the excitement of the ball, and not enough sleep, and now this piece of news all combined. Caroline is quite well, and she will feel much better after a nap."

"No," said Caroline automatically, "I cannot sleep now, I must—"

Somewhere in her mind she fixed upon the fact that she must find Stuart. She must talk with him about this, he must know what she is thinking, now they had both slept on it.

There had been little time for conversation yesterday. It had all been so hurried, so frantic, so…untamed. She'd had to return home, and they had agreed to discuss it later.

Later. Later when? They could not take back what they had done, and in Caroline's darkest heart, she had no wish to.

To experience such pleasure with another…to discover one's body was capable of feeling such things…

"Sleep," said her Mama firmly.

Caroline shook her head. "No, I must—"

But her mother was having none of it. "Nonsense," she said briskly. "Mrs. Castle!"

Bustling into the room as though she was always just behind the door when they needed her came Mrs. Castle. Her features softened when she saw the red eyes and tearstained cheeks.

"Mrs. Castle, Miss Caroline needs hot cocoa and *rest*."

From where Caroline sat, it sounded as though everything was happening from very far away. The voices around her traveled through a tunnel to reach her, growing muffled on the way.

She allowed herself to be led out of the room and up the stairs, by exactly who she was unsure. Two pairs of hands helped her into bed and rested a blanket over her, while another pair closed the curtains to prevent the thin streams of December daylight getting through. All was done in silence, and as the last pair of footsteps walked out of the room and the door was shut behind them, Caroline breathed out and closed her eyes. Just for a moment.

Which was why it was such a surprise when she opened her eyes and saw, according to the small traveling clock Esther had won in a raffle two Easters ago, that it was now three o'clock. In the afternoon?

Caroline started. *Surely she could not have slept for so long?*

But after rising and tapping the front of the clock, she could see it was still ticking—and as she drew the curtains back from the window, the sun had definitely moved in the sky.

I must have been more tired than I realized, thought Caroline, *to sleep for so long in the middle of the day.*

Looking down, she saw her beautiful cream gown which had been so carefully ironed—under the watchful eye of Mrs. Castle by a poor housemaid, no doubt—had become wrinkled and creased as she had slept.

But it did not matter. Nothing mattered. *Not now she and Stuart had…*

It was strange. Caroline had traversed one of the greatest rules of Society—to keep that sort of lovemaking for the marriage bed.

Yet she felt no guilt. What they had shared…it was wonderful. It should be celebrated. It was sacred between them, yet she would not change it for the world.

All she would change was Stuart's indecision about whether to marry her. And the lack of a French letter, which he had sheepishly showed her before she had slipped out of his rooms.

Caroline swallowed. *The thought that she could have given her innocence to a gentleman who may, in the end, not choose to make her his wife...*

There was no one she could talk to about this; no one but Stuart.

At this time of day, he was usually doing his rounds to the countless people who waited for his knock to comfort them in their infirmities or medicate them in their sickness, but he was often finished by three o'clock in the afternoon. He took his rest when he could, he always said, for he may up in the night several times if his patients required him.

If she made haste, she could be at his lodgings, waiting for him when he returned.

Caroline had slept fully clothed, so all it took was a quick rearrangement of her hair pins and slipping on a pair of pearl earbobs to make her suitable for public viewing. Wild flame curls threatened to fall down her neck, so despite her haste, it took her a few minutes of adjusting until she was happy.

Her pelisse was in the hallway, but she could hear Mrs. Castle berating a housemaid there, so she decided to walk out of the house through the garden, then out through the side gate.

The last thing that she wanted to face now was more questions.

It did not take her long to reach Stuart's lodgings, and thankfully the sun was shining. It did not look as though it would snow again today. Though his landlady was visible through the window into the front room, Caroline managed to slip up the backstairs and dropped into the chair at his desk.

If only she could prevent her thoughts from wildly growing out into all directions. If only waiting for Stuart could be over in a minute.

Thankfully, she did not have to wait long. Before the bells around London had announced that it was half-past three, heavy footsteps pounded up the stairs, and Stuart burst into the room.

"Caroline," he said, rushing toward her and kneeling at her

feet. "My landlady mentioned before she went out of tea that she heard footsteps and thought a shy patient may be waiting here for me—you rushed away yesterday so quickly I did not have any time to—"

"I know," said Caroline quietly. "I think that when…when the enormity of what we had done hit me, I had to leave. I needed to think."

Stuart rose to take off his hat and greatcoat. "The enormity of what we had done?"

"I…" Caroline swallowed. *She would be mistress of herself.* "I still cannot believe, in many ways, that we really and truly made love—and yet the memory of it is so…strong."

"Oh," said Stuart shortly. "I did not know you felt that way about it."

There was pain in his voice, and Caroline could not fathom why.

"Stuart, I do not regret that we made love yesterday."

His head snapped up. "You do not?"

With a weary smile, Caroline said, "No. I will admit I had not expected to make love—not fully—before we were married, but the idea something so beautiful, so intensely pleasurable, could be regretted… No, I do not regret that we made love."

"But the way you speak," said Stuart slowly, "makes me think you regret something."

Discomfort rushed through her. How could she put it into words…

"I will admit," she said, trying to force down her nausea, "the idea I could be with child right now, sitting here talking to you, is one that fills me with a powerful sense of fear and uncertainty."

Stuart stared. She had expected him to speak in that moment, reassure her, comfort her—even perhaps admit he was a little fearful himself.

But the more he sat in silence, the worse Caroline began to feel.

"Stuart!" She eventually broke the silence. "You are looking at me as if you do not even know me!"

"Do I?" Stuart shot back. "I had always thought…when we talked about the future, you always said you wanted to have children. We agreed we wanted a family of our own."

That was his fear? Caroline could hardly believe it. Had the man entirely forgotten his mother's words? Had he blanked out the mortifying suggestion Mrs. Walsingham had made, and in public, too?

"My wishes have not changed," she said firmly. "You cannot think I am so changeable! I still want a family, I still want to create that family with you. But not like this. Not unwed, still unsure whether…whether or not that wedding will take place!"

She had intended her last remark to force him into making a statement. *Yes, it was happening, of course I'll marry you, something of that nature.*

But he said nothing.

"Stuart?"

"You cannot possibly know," said Stuart, his voice low and dull. "You cannot possibly know if you are with child yet. As a doctor, neither can I. We will have to wait and see."

It was such an inadequate response to her fears that Caroline felt a spark of irritation around her heart.

And that was supposed to be her solace? That was supposed to make her feel better?

Where was the man she had fallen in love with? Where was the gentleman who had fought through poverty to give his mother and sister a better life? Where was the Stuart who loved her?

She stood up. "And that is all you can say to me? Nothing about whether or not we are to be married? Nothing about your mother who has changed her mind about me? Who despite preparing herself to welcome me as a daughter, now believes me unsuitable for you? No words of comfort about how you will always love me and support me if I am truly with child?"

"Dammit, Caroline!" Stuart suddenly exploded, his hands

clenched as he took an unsteady step toward her. "You know I love you more than anything in this damn world, but if my father, in the few short years that he was alive and I knew him, taught me anything, it is that responsibilities have to be met. Do you think it won't tear me apart to lose you? Do you think I agree with all my mother says?"

"At some point you'll have to choose!" Walking toward him, Caroline placed her left hand over his heart. In that instant, she knew precisely what she had to say. "I can feel your heartbeat, Stuart, and it beats with mine. My hand holds the ring you gave me when you asked me to be your wife, and I'll be damned if I'm going to lose you."

Stuart growled in his throat, and after placing his hand over hers, swiftly pulled her into his arms and swept her into a kiss. His tongue, not gentle and slow this time, was forceful yet desperate. Desperate perhaps to show her with action what he could not do in words.

Caroline could not help herself—she wound her arms around his neck and succumbed completely. Her anger and frustration did not dissipate, but her love for him was still the strongest emotion within her.

Though something else was growing, something strong and deep that stirred her, causing hot throbs to pulsate through her body.

"No, Stuart," Caroline pulled away, though it was the hardest thing she had ever done. She looked into his eyes, wild and gazing into her own. "We must not—not again."

"What difference does it make?" Stuart whispered. "We have made love already, do you think it will make much difference if we do again?"

"But what if I am not with child now?"

Stuart said in a low voice, "The thought of you carrying my child makes me want to make love to you even more, Caroline. My landlady has gone out, there is no one else in the building. We…we are all alone, able to be as loud and as joyful as we wish.

By God, woman, you've set me on fire, and I know of only one way to quench the flames."

Caroline acted on pure instinct, without any thought.

Raising her partly open lips to his, her hands moved from his neck, past his chest, and down to that area she was only just starting to know. Her fingers were hesitant at first, but at the sight of Stuart's eyes closing in pleasure and hearing the groans emanating from his mouth, she became more daring.

The slightest touch of her fingers to Stuart's manhood through his breeches caused it to twitch, to swell, and within minutes, Caroline wondered whether he was ready. Ready to enter her and bring her to such gratifying peaks as he had before.

But not yet.

Stuart wrenched himself from her and said unevenly, "Time to get these clothes off you."

It did not take them long to strip to their skin, and their restraint did not last.

Unlike the last time, when they had ventured down untrodden paths and explored a bright new world together, now they knew the height of climax, the peaks of intimacy they could reach, and had no wish to wait.

Caroline gasped as his hands moved to cup her buttocks, arching her back as he lowered his mouth to tease at her breasts.

"Stuart," she moaned, "I want you now!"

She had not intended this. No thought of seducing each other once again had entered her heart before she had gone to his lodgings.

But Caroline was not thinking now, only feeling.

"I know, but you need to be patient," he said, lifting his head for a moment. "There is so much that I want you to experience—and this is only the beginning."

The beginning? Caroline could barely think, but the little concentration she had wondered what else they could possibly enjoy, when they were already sharing such bliss?

But Stuart had other ideas. After kissing her passionately once more, he took her hands and led her to his bed.

"Lie down," he said in a voice that seemed just about under control. Caroline did so, but when she reached out an arm, inviting him down to her, he shook his head. "Now shut your eyes."

"Stuart," she protested, "why?"

He smiled as he moved to stand at the end of the bed. "You'll see."

Everything in her was desperate to make love to Stuart again—even if it was for one last time. Her eyelids fluttered down.

Now she could not see anything, all other senses heightened. She could hear something which must be Stuart moving.

"Oh God, Caroline," breathed Stuart. "Everything in me urges me to sink myself into you right now."

Caroline shivered. It sounded as though he was resisting, though she did not know why. She wanted him.

But nothing happened.

And then everything happened. The most intense crest of sensuality washed through her like a wave. She could not help but cry out in joy as soft wet lips placed themselves right upon her secret place. Stuart's hands were on her thighs as he gently pushed them apart, giving his mouth better access.

"Stuart, wh-what—" Caroline could barely construct a sentence, the intensity of the feelings was so overwhelming.

She could not see what was happening, keeping her eyes shut as instructed, but she felt his lips leave her body and twitched in unconscious disappointment.

"Just relax," said Stuart's voice, "and delight in what you are about to feel…"

CHAPTER EIGHT

A WEEK LATER, Caroline awoke to a harsh stabbing pain near her hip.

She looked down and saw the sheets stained with blood.

"No," she whispered under her breath, almost unsure exactly why—then another stabbing pain flowed through her stomach, and she clutched at it, biting her bottom lip to prevent herself from waking Jemima.

This was not new, after all, Caroline thought frantically. Her monthly cycle was something she had endured for many years now, and it was not uncommon for one of her sisters to awaken to find the stain of blood marking their sheets.

But now...

"No, no, no." Caroline did not seem to know how to stop as she rose unsteadily from the bed.

The answer to the question she had been torturing herself with for the last week had been answered swiftly.

Caroline had expected relief to swiftly follow this discovery, yet she felt none. Instead, she just felt emptiness, a slightly sick feeling of something akin to disappointment.

The last few days she and Stuart had agreed not to see each other. It was too painful, too confusing. Decisions had to be made, decisions he had assured her he could not make with her continuous presence.

Which was precisely what Caroline was afraid of. If she allowed herself to be removed from his presence, would he not become accustomed to her absence? Would he believe it easy, moving through the world as the Earl of Cheshire, rather than plain old Dr. Walsingham, with a well-bred but untitled wife on his arm?

Almost without thinking, Caroline moved quietly over to the place where she and Jemima kept the special linens they required for their cycle. Her habits, forged from years of dealing with the exact same circumstances, carried her through the next ten minutes, but by the time she was finished, she was left once again with her own thoughts, feelings—confusion.

She had not expected this. The pain, yes, that was always an accompanying factor with her monthly cycle—something Jemima had never suffered. Even the ache within her hips was something she often experienced, although it was particularly harsh today.

But the feelings of loss, sadness, almost mourning for the child which, deep in her heart, Caroline had been sure had been there…that was entirely new.

She stifled a sob as she stood, knees almost buckling under the pain.

Jemima stirred.

Caroline, desperate not to have to answer any questions, quickly moved across the room and tried to open the door quietly. She picked up her robe on the way and wrapped it around her. Within a moment, she was on the stairs going down to the library.

The library. It was where Caroline always gravitated to when suffering the pains of her monthly cycle. If she could avoid using laudanum, of course, that was all the better.

Crawling into an armchair, Caroline tucked her legs underneath her and brought up her knees, relieving the tension in her stomach.

Despite the early hour, there was already a fire ablaze in the grate. Something Mrs. Castle always approved of was fires in winter, something Caroline was beyond thankful for.

She stretched her hands toward the fire, thought of the child that had not been, and wept.

The next day, despite the continuing pain, Caroline was calmer.

Forced to stay in bed for an entire day by her concerned mother once she had been discovered in the library, and frustrated at hearing the celebrations of Jemima's engagement—*to a man I have never met*, she thought bitterly, *and it is not as though anyone bothered to explain exactly how this man wormed his way into our family*—Caroline was determined to be up and about, regardless of what her mother said.

When she traipsed downstairs the next day, however, the rest of the family had already breakfasted, and her father was just about to leave, pulling on his huge greatcoat in the hallway.

"Ah, Caroline my dear," he said, waving away Mrs. Castle who was trying to encourage him to wear a second scarf around his neck—*"because it's an awful wind out there, sir, and the last thing I need is a sick house at Christmas"*— "A letter came for you early this morning, and after recognizing young Walsingham's hand, I thought it best to pass it on to you as early as possible."

"Thank you, Papa."

Caroline smiled just to see the beloved handwriting on the outside of the parchment. Stuart. Just knowing his hand had held this paper, she felt closer to him. Pulling it open, she saw only a few words.

I will call for you at eleven o'clock. I hope you are feeling re-stored to your vibrant self.

Caroline could not help but smile. *If there was one thing she gained from being engaged to be married to a doctor*, she thought, *it was that he truly understood the complexities of the female condition during her monthly cycle.*

Stuart had never expected her to be as normal, sympathized with the pain, and had even forgiven a few tempers which had managed to escape her control over the years.

"Good news, I hope?"

Caroline looked up to see her Papa waiting on the doorstep, door latch in hand, looking at her expectantly.

She nodded with a smile. "Dr. Walsingham will be calling to see me at eleven o'clock, Papa—I hope that is quite suitable?"

Her father laughed. "Who am I to say nay to the fifteenth Earl of Cheshire?"

He pulled the door shut, so no one saw Caroline's smile falter.

Of course. In the pain and sadness she had felt about not carrying Stuart's child, it was easy to push his new title to the side of her mind.

Now she could not. Now her mind was flooded with the reminder Stuart's mother was entirely against their marriage.

Caroline popped her head into the library to see exactly what the time was, and saw from the gold gilt clock on the mantel that it was already ten minutes to eleven. She had little time, if any, to prepare herself. But as she did not know exactly why Stuart was coming, she supposed it made little difference. She was already dressed, choosing today a lighter cream gown with a burgundy braid along the hem and the sleeves. What else was she to do?

As ALWAYS, STUART was punctual. In fact, he had arrived a few minutes early but had spent that time staring at the Fitzroys' front door. The knocker, one now familiar to him, was only inches away, yet he did not lift it.

Stuart sighed, letting out a huge breath that blossomed in the cold air.

What was he doing here? What was he to do?

Despite trying to visit Caroline yesterday to talk about the situation—*my situation*, he reminded himself bitterly—he had been told the several times he had called that she was unwell and not to be disturbed.

If he were not predisposed to believe Mrs. Castle, who guarded the young Fitzroy girls better than she did her own kitchen, Stuart would have suspected he was being kept away.

It was too much to believe they were still unaware of his rise to nobility, and though he hoped against it with every sinew in his body, he was unsure if they were aware of his mother's opinion on the matter.

Stuart stamped his feet to keep the cold from creeping into his boots. Clenching his hands inside the large pockets of his greatcoat, he took a deep breath. *This was ridiculous.* He needed to speak to Caroline.

A short rap with the knocker was all that was required. If he could bring himself to do it.

Stuart coughed into his hands, shook his shoulders, and reached out a hand. He knocked. He waited.

The smiling and welcoming face of Mrs. Castle appeared, but the expression swiftly fell. "Good morning, Dr. Wal—I mean, your lord…your worshipful Earl of—"

"My dear Mrs. Castle," interrupted Stuart, a shadow passing across his face. *Damn, why was every conversation like this now?* "I am the same Dr. Walsingham you have greeted at this very doorstep for a long time, and I would not want anything to change that."

Mrs. Castle looked aghast at treating him just like any other man. "But sir—my *lord!*"

"But nothing." Stuart's voice was firm as he stepped into the warmth. Despite Mrs. Castle's protests, he took his own greatcoat off and asked one simple question. "Where is she?"

Mrs. Castle's eyes betrayed her before her mouth could even open, and Stuart did not wait for verbal confirmation. Two strides were all that was needed to make his way to the library door.

"Stuart!"

The voice came from one of the armchairs from the fire, and

Stuart quickly moved around to it and saw—Caroline. She was curled up in the armchair with a rug over her knees.

The tension in Stuart's shoulders dissipated.

"I am relieved," he confessed, sinking into the armchair opposite her without taking his eyes from her face. "Not only because it is far too long without seeing your face, but because I can see from one look you have truly been unwell. It does me such good to know you have not been kept from me—or have been keeping away from me."

It was a long speech and a foolish one, now Stuart came to think of it. Not very gentlemanly to be relieved a woman had been unwell. *And why would the Fitzroys wish to keep Caroline away from him? They were far more likely to be pushing her toward him…*

He regretted the unkind thought immediately. He had known the Fitzroys for months. Was he really so quick to believe them callous and mercenary?

"Keeping away from you?" Caroline smiled weakly. "It is your mother who wants to keep you away from me."

Stuart's jaw clenched, but decided to let that remark go. "How are you feeling, Caroline?"

"Not at my peak, I will admit," said Caroline with a quiet laugh. "But please do not concern yourself Stuart, honestly—it is only…" But her voice broke.

"Caroline!" Stuart dropped from his chair to kneel on the floor beside her as fear gripped his heart. *Something truly awful must have happened.*

"I am sorry." It was clear Caroline was trying desperately not to let the tears welling up fall onto her cheeks. "It is but my…my monthly cycle."

Stuart nodded knowledgably. "I know it can be overwhelming, this time for you, but I do not believe I have ever seen you weep because of it. Talk to me, what else is going on?"

His gaze raked over her. She looked pale, yes, as though she had not slept through the night in many days…but this had never caused tears in her before.

Caroline shook her head as she looked at the bookcase opposite her, at the fire, at the ceiling, anywhere but at him. "I know it is strange—I know I have been worried that I was... was with child," and here she lowered her voice, despite the fact that they were the only two in the room. "And now I know I am not with child I should feel some sort of relief, or gratitude..."

Stuart had never seen her so bereft of calm, so lost in the emotions sweeping through her.

"...yet I will admit," Caroline continued, her gaze finally meeting his as one single tear fell onto her cheek, "I do feel a sense of loss, for it means I may never now have any chance of carrying your child."

Oh, hell.

Stuart sighed and dropped his gaze. "I had not considered it in that way," he said quietly. "I will confess, in my turn, the idea my child," and now he moved to place a hand on Caroline's cheek, his thumb brushing away the tear, "my son or daughter," and the hand dropped to rest, gently, upon Caroline's stomach, "could have been growing here...it made parts of me stir I did not even know that I had."

A soft sob escaped Caroline. As difficult as it had been to admit that, even to the one he loved, the next part of the conversation was to be harder.

Perhaps impossible.

"My love," Stuart said gently, offering her his handkerchief which she took willingly. "You must know we have not just lost the one and only chance we will ever have for a family."

"Maybe not," said Caroline, and there was an element of steel in her tones. "But if your mother has her way, there will be no chance at all."

Stuart groaned. "Caroline, can we just leave that for—"

"Leave it?" Caroline struggled to sit more upright, looking him full in the face. "You think I can just forget your mother told me in public that she does not want our marriage to take place? That is not an easy thing to forget!"

"Caroline," Stuart spoke with little idea how to calm her, but the fire in her eyes made him sit back in the armchair behind him. "It is so much more complex than that, you know it is."

"Do I?" Her words were sharp, but there were no tears in Caroline's eyes now. "My word, then I am shamefully ill-informed. I was under the impression you had just inherited a title, you would now have to live somewhere else with a completely different occupation than the one you have trained for, and had been told by your mother—your only living parent—that you were forbidden from marrying the woman you had already proposed to. One she already did not like. What a strange coincidence."

Stuart tried not to focus on the fact that the more passionate Caroline became, the more her bosom heaved up and down as she spoke.

Concentrate on the facts, man.

"My mother—" he began.

"Your mother," said Caroline calmly, "is a woman I greatly admire—nay, I would even say I like her. But people I like, even people I love, can be wrong. Your mother is wrong."

"Money does not just come from nowhere, Caroline," Stuart said helplessly, throwing up his hands and sinking back in the armchair. "I am required to find fifty thousand pounds—do you have any ideas where I can pluck it from the ground?"

Caroline's jaw dropped. "Fifty thousand pounds?"

He nodded. Nausea and pain in his head returned, the same sensations from when he had first heard that figure come out of the mouth of the accountant who had traveled all the way from Cheshire.

Fifty thousand pounds. Such a sum.

"Fifty thousand pounds," repeated Caroline in a hushed tone, eyes wide. "It is hard to imagine such a sum! And that is the debt upon the estate?"

"It is more," said Stuart weightily, "but that is the sum that will bring us close to being able to pay our most insistent debts."

It hurt Stuart to see the woman he wanted so desperately to become his wife look at him in horror. *Who could have guessed that rising to such noble heights could sink him to such painful depths?*

"But," she said quietly, "it is not as though it is your debt! You did not create it—why should you pay it?"

"It does not work that way," Stuart spoke darkly. "You know that. I am learning more and more about it with each passing day. The debt was not of my Great Uncle Edward, but of the Earldom of Cheshire itself. It was made upon that basis, and the Earldom of Cheshire still exists, just as it did when the debt was made."

Caroline opened her eyes wide as she considered. "What could your Great Uncle have spent it all on?"

Stuart laughed bitterly. "You think this was all spent by one man? Oh, no. Apparently the earldom has been in debt for some four generations—and with each earl who does not pay, the interest merely accumulates and passes on to the next unsuspecting victim."

"But I have never heard of this," Caroline said fiercely, as though she was regularly kept informed about the debts of earls. "Perhaps there is a mistake."

"No one of noble rank would ever admit to such a debt," said Stuart quietly. "No one of honor would. I never would, and I never will, save to those who are close to me."

Caroline sighed and turned to look into the fire. Stuart wished he could peer inside that mind and understand what she was thinking. *Could she conceive of a solution?* He could not.

"Do not forget," he said heavily, "I am in a small way responsible for at least some of the debt."

Caroline's head shot round as she exclaimed, "Surely not!"

"Who was it that paid the tuition and bills for my medical training?" Stuart said with sad smile. "I had never known, until my mother informed me at our engagement ball."

"Your mysterious benefactor."

It was all he could do not to smile. It had all seemed so convenient—he had never bothered to find out more. Why should he? The fees were paid, half his rent, a little money to his mother…why would one inquire into something so expedient?

Well, he was paying the price now.

"It was your Great Uncle, all along."

Stuart opened his arms wide. "Precisely."

Silence fell between them.

As Caroline continued to gaze pensively into the fire, Stuart could not take his eyes from her. Every aspect of her: he wanted to commit every inch to memory so that in the future when he needed to imagine perfection, he already had the blueprint.

The slope of her nose and those beautiful lips, the hair almost as much an inferno as the fire in the grate that her beautiful gray eyes watched. The curve of her breasts as they fell over that sumptuous waist, parts of her he could not see at this moment but had tasted and worshipped—and thought he always would.

But there was no point in putting off the inevitable, no chance to avoid the conversation, no escape from the words he was about to speak. He had to speak.

Stuart cleared his throat. "My mother has issued an ultimatum."

DESPITE HER FATIGUE, a spark of anger flowed through Caroline. "An ultimatum?"

It was as though Stuart could already tell he had made a mistake. "Well, when I say ultimatum, what I really mean is—"

"Don't mollycoddle me, Stuart," she said bitterly. "I mean, it is not as though we had agreed to spend the rest of our lives together! I would not want you to think you need to keep things from me, or twist your words to ensure I am not offended."

"Damnit, Caroline, you think this is easy?" exploded Stuart. "I have my mother on one side, the woman who bore me, loved me, cared for me, supported me even when she lost my father and struggled with two young children! On the other, the woman who stirs me and whom I love! I want to cast myself at your feet every time I look at you because I am so ridiculously in love with you!"

"Well at some point you'll have to choose!" Caroline rose from the armchair.

An anchor felt tied around her ankle keeping her close to Stuart, but she had to move, she could not just sit there and listen to him without doing something.

Had she ever thought he would be faced with such a choice? Had she ever imagined she would be the one making him choose?

But no, Caroline reminded herself fiercely. It was Mrs. Walsingham who was making him choose, Mrs. Walsingham who had suggested an ultimatum.

And Stuart, trapped between them.

She took a deep breath. "Everyone has to make a choice at some point in their marriage, Stuart. At some point there will be a collision of opinions between parents and spouses, and you have to choose."

"Choose?" Stuart looked at her wildly. "I do not think you could be so blasé about this if you were having to choose between me and your mother!"

"I…" Caroline spluttered, turning her back to him. *How dare he bring her mother in this!* "That is beside the point!"

"No."

Caroline could tell from his voice that Stuart was moving toward her. Sure enough, his arm grabbed hers and turned her so they were face to face.

It was difficult to remember she was angry with him when she looked into his eyes. All she wanted to do was to fall into his arms and be comforted by him.

Why could he not see how desperately she needed him?

"No," repeated Stuart. "You know full well it is not beside the point. I am in an impossible situation, one I would not wish on my worst enemy." Taking her hands in his own, he lowered his voice and said, "But if you sit with me, I will explain what she said, and you can tell me your thoughts."

Caroline glared suspiciously. "Why do I get the feeling I am not going to like the terms of this so-called ultimatum?"

"Because you will not," said Stuart frankly, raising her hands to his lips and kissing them. "But you have to hear them."

Sighing, Caroline knew she had little choice. "Charmer."

Despite the aching pain in her stomach, she could not deny his logic. It would be foolish not to listen to what Mrs. Walsingham had said to her son.

How else would she be able to argue against it?

Caroline allowed herself to be led back to her armchair. Relaxing as she sat, she could feel the pain and tension disappearing. At least, that which resided in her chest.

"Better?" Stuart gave her a knowing look, and Caroline could not help but return it with a roll of her eyes.

"You know it is," she said argumentatively. "And I have not forgotten what I am about to hear. Come on, then. What did your mother say?"

Stuart swallowed and sat slowly in the armchair opposite her. "You must not think my mother does not like you. If anything, she is suffering the most from—"

"If you try to convince me," said Caroline darkly, "that she is the one suffering, or that she ever liked me—for you know she did not—I will get up, walk out of this room, go to my bed, and instruct Mrs. Castle to be most forthright with you if you ever decide to call here again."

Stuart laughed despite himself. "I knew there was a reason I fell in love with you."

"One of many," Caroline said, smiling despite herself. "Now, tell me plainly. What is your mother's ultimatum to me?"

Stuart shook his head slowly. "To you? Oh no, my mother is much more direct. The ultimatum is for me. She told me last night that I had a simple choice. I could either break ties with you completely, promise to never see you again, and begin to make overtures to a young Right Honorable Miss Ursula Blakemoor, who I am informed is a young woman of thirty thousand pounds, and a sickly younger brother upon whose death she would inherit another twenty thousand, or…"

But here his voice trailed off.

Caroline stared, concern lining her face. "Or?"

Stuart rubbed at his temples. "Or," he said finally, "I could marry you. I will be penniless, be forced to sell off the estate, abandon thousands to the poorhouse, reduce my sister's prospects, and condemn my mother to a life of penury in her old age."

Caroline's eyes widened as she gazed in shock. It took several full minutes of complete silence, save the clock chiming, for her to fully comprehend what she had just heard.

That a woman could say such a thing, and to her own child…that money was so valuable that it would supersede the life, the happiness of her child…

And yet, she was not wrong. Caroline bit her lip. It would be easy to wave away the consequences of such an action, but though she and Mrs. Walsingham appeared to agree on little else, Caroline could not ignore the numerous people who would suffer from such a connection.

A connection such as their marriage.

"I…I have a dowry," she said quietly.

Stuart smiled genially. "Is it fifty thousand pounds?"

"No," Caroline said with a wry smile. "No, it is three thousand."

But as she spoke, an idea occurred to her. Well, it had been three thousand two years ago, when she had first entered Society, her mother had made a point of mentioning it.

Was there a chance it was higher—that her father's investments may have grown?

"And so that is the choice I face!" Stuart threw his arms up in the air. "Apparently it happens! Titles, just dropping down on a man's head, with all the responsibility it entails. And you know, simply because I was not born to this way of life, with this rank I now have thrust upon me, I am now held to those high standards!

God, if you could comprehend half of the pressure on me now—"

"I do understand," said Caroline, reaching out a hand to comfort him, mind racing. She must speak to her father as soon as possible.

But Stuart pushed past her hand as he paced around the room. "How could you!" His voice was sharp. "I was at Windsor Castle yesterday afternoon swearing allegiance to the Prince Regent!"

Caroline stared. No, she must have heard that incorrectly. He could not have said—

"Windsor Castle?" she said weakly, watching Stuart pace up and down the library like a caged animal. *Prince Regent?*

"That is my life now!" Stuart paused before the mantel and laughed mirthlessly. "And I have to return to him tomorrow to ascertain my abilities to support the court financially in times of war, and to make official notice of any women I am courting!"

Caroline stepped to him, hesitantly. "That is ridiculous, Stuart, they cannot expect you to—"

"How do you know?" Stuart spoke harshly. "You know nothing of this world, even less than I—which is saying something. How can you help me navigate this, how can you support me in situations you could have only dreamed of?"

"I don't know," said Caroline helplessly. "But I will try, I will do my best to—"

"And this issue with my mother does not help," continued Stuart bitterly. "It is the last thing that I need right now!"

Every word stung Caroline's heart. "Perhaps it would just be easier if I weren't here!"

"Perhaps it would be easier if we did not get married!"

The words spoken by Stuart erupted into silence. Caroline watched a war of emotions on his face, always shifting, never settling. Anger, confusion, panic at the responsibilities he was now to shoulder, hung in the air around them.

Both Caroline and Stuart stood still, but nothing could take back his words.

"Right." Caroline did not move, nothing of her moved save

her lips. "I see."

Stuart stared, seemingly unable to speak, move, do anything.

Caroline waited. *Say something,* she begged him silently. *Take it back. Tell me you love me. Tell me that we will get through this together. Tell me anything.*

The clock chimed. It was twelve o'clock. And Stuart said not a word.

Caroline took a deep breath. She could not wait forever. She could not expect Stuart to abandon his family for her—after all, he had a point. Would she do the same for him?

Her mind flittered through her sisters, her mother, even her Papa, a man who was not her blood but had raised her as a daughter.

Could she abandon them at the drop of a hat? Would she agree to leave them forever to be with Stuart?

Her heart warred, pulled between two great loves, and she understood what Stuart was enduring.

Agony.

She would not allow him to tear himself apart to make the decision. She would not be the reason he lost all respect for himself, why others suffered, why his mother would be forced into destitution.

It was impossible choice. And she would make it for him.

"Mrs. Castle will see you out," she said, pulling off the diamond engagement ring which had felt so right on her finger. She placed it on the arm of the chair.

She had swept past him and reached the door of the library before Stuart even had a chance to move.

"Caroline, wait!"

She did wait, but only to stand in the doorway and have one last look at him before she walked out of his life forever. "I am worth more than any earldom. And I can see that I am not, not worth the happiness of thousands. I fell in love with Dr. Walsingham, but...but he is gone. I suggest you call upon Miss Blakemoor. I imagine she will wish to marry the Earl of Cheshire."

CHAPTER NINE

IT WAS CHRISTMAS Day, a day for celebration and laughter. Caroline could not remember being so miserable.

"Merry Christmas, my darling daughters!" Her Papa moved forward to accept the smiles and embraces of his children as his wife sat on the chaise longue and laughed.

Just like every other year he had decided to dress up as Father Christmas, and his green lined jacket and breeches had been retrimmed by Mrs. Castle with a little white fur.

Caroline's first memory of Christmas was snuggling up with her stepfather as the family sang songs together around a very old and out of tune pianoforte. No wonder none of them had good singing voices.

As she had gained more sisters over the years, their gaiety soon included parlor games, sweet treats, visiting friends who lived nearby with children of a similar age.

She had such fond memories of those times, and it seemed a shame that this year, her memory of Christmas was going to be of melancholy.

"Why the sad face, Caroline?" Arabella was seated on the rug by the fire with Sophia, the two of them roasting chestnuts. "Will you not join us?"

Caroline shook her head, not bothering to attempt to speak over the excitement from the center of the room.

"It is as though she has raised me back to life!" The tall man with dark hair spoke clearly, his gaze unwavering from Jemima. "Without her, I would still be dead."

"Nonsense," Jemima spoke sharply but with a smile.

Her stepsister's hand was encircled by the man beside her. He was wearing a form of military uniform Caroline recognized—perhaps from her engagement ball?

Jemima had chosen her scarlet silk gown. They were matched perfectly. "You were fine before I found you. I have just improved you, somewhat!"

The two of them laughed, along with Caroline's mother. "Oh, it does my heart good to see you laugh, Jemima. I must thank you, Captain Rotherham, for putting it there!"

Their laughter was innocent, but to the pained Caroline's heart, as though they were scraping fingernails down a blackboard.

They could not possibly know what had occurred between her and Stuart three days before—a benefit of lining a room with books was that no sound escaped it—and it was most difficult to see two people so obviously in love.

So happy. With their future before them.

Seated alone on the sofa opposite the window, Caroline looked at her stepsister: watched her smile broaden as Captain Rotherham whispered something in her ear, watched their clasped hands tighten, her sister beaming as though she did not have a care in the world.

It was certainly a new Jemima. Although Caroline was glad of it, she could not help but marvel at how her previous happiness with Stuart must have crushed Jemima.

Now she knew exactly what it was like to look in from the outside into happiness.

Jemima and Captain Rotherham's engagement was swift, certainly, but neither Caroline nor the rest of her family had any doubts they were besotted with each other. It would be a happy union.

Caroline's eyes flickered, unbidden, to the window. Despite everything, she still carried some small hope Stuart would arrive suddenly, knocking on the door, ready to come in and sweep her off her feet. Declare it had all been some terrible mistake and he was not going to be the earl after all, and he still wanted to marry her because he loved her—

"Caroline?"

Her Papa's voice brought her back into the room. He was seated beside her, although she had not noticed him sit down. His gaze was full of concern.

"Caroline, are you well?"

Caroline forced the smile she had practiced in the looking glass. "Quite well, thank you Papa."

"Hmmph." Her father did not look convinced, but thankfully there was too much to distract him from her happiness—or lack thereof.

"Papa, do you want some roast chestnuts?" Sophia's voice called across the room, and Caroline sighed with relief. She could do without questions, but she would not escape them forever.

More's the pity.

"Caroline, when does Stuart arrive?" Jemima looked over with a smile. "I want to introduce him to Hugh."

Caroline opened her mouth, but to her absolute horror, no sound came out.

"Caroline?" Never before had Jemima's voice been so hesitant. "Caroline, do you feel unwell?"

"I knew there was something wrong," said her Papa, raising his hand to her forehead and looking into her eyes with concern. "Why did you not tell us you were not feeling well, Caroline?"

"I am well!" Caroline rose from the sofa, unable to bear it.

A quick look around the room told her she had raised, if possible, more concern than alleviating it. She sighed, preparing herself to say the words that had to be uttered.

As long as she spoke slowly and clearly, she would get the words out. Then hopefully the rest of them would leave her alone.

"Stuart—Dr. Walsing…the earl and I are no longer engaged. Our understanding is at an end, and I do not expect to see him again."

The silence that filled the room was only broken by the sound of the chestnuts roasting on the fire.

Eventually, Sophia spoke in a small voice. "Not ever again?"

Caroline swallowed. "No."

"Darling child, when did this happen?" Her Mama rushed over to her and lifted up Caroline's head with a finger under her chin. "Why did you not tell me?"

"I can make him come back." Her Papa stood to his full height, and despite his comical costume, there was fire in his expression. "Do not concern yourself Caroline, we shall make sure he honors the promises he made to you! To think he can come here, expect to be welcome in this family—"

"What happened, Caroline?" Arabella had moved from the fire, leaving Sophia trying to hold back tears. "What did he do to make you change your mind?"

"Nothing," choked Caroline, the well of emotion she had tried desperately to dam flowing once more. "And I do not want to have a bad word spoken against him, I would much rather forget that it ever happened, and—"

"Months!" Her father exploded. "Months and months of courting, of having you believe, us all believe—that is not something I can forget, I will not forgive! Worming himself into this family, taking the happiness of my child away—and at Christmas! What a despicable, low, ungentlemanly—"

"Papa," Caroline interrupted hastily. Oh, she could not bear to have this conversation here, right where anyone could hear them! "May I speak to you, please? In your study?"

For a moment, she thought he was about to refuse, but perhaps he saw the anguish in her eyes. With a jerk of his head, her father left the room.

Caroline stepped out of the drawing room and across the hall into her Papa's study without looking at any of her family. How could she?

"Well," her father said heavily as she shut the door behind her. "What is this all about, then?"

Caroline swallowed and tried to smile at her father, who was leaning in his Father Christmas garb on his desk. "It all started with the ball, I suppose."

"Ball?"

"The man who died," Caroline clarified. *Oh, this was so much more difficult than she had expected.* "He was Stuart's—"

"Yes, yes, the earl who died and made Stuart earl in his place," said her Papa, waving a hand. "We know all that."

Caroline took a deep breath. "What you don't know is that…that the earldom is in debt."

The words echoed in the silence, and when she looked up to catch her father's eye, she saw dawning understanding.

"Ah."

She nodded wretchedly. "And you see, my dowry isn't suffi-cient to—"

"And how would you know that?"

Caroline blinked. Her father had that irritating knowing smile he sometimes had when he was about to win at cards.

"Your dowry," her Papa said slowly, "is a mite different from when we last spoke."

Hope, small but powerful, leapt in Caroline's heart. *She had wondered!* "But it cannot be—"

"Enough? Oh, I wouldn't know that," said her Papa with a grin. "But I think many people wouldn't say no to thirty thousand pounds."

It was a good thing there was a chair directly behind her, or else Caroline may well have fallen to the floor, knees giving way.

Thirty thousand—thirty thousand pounds? Her?

Why, that made her an heiress!

Caroline's thoughts rushed through her mind hastily. It was not the desired fifty thousand, of course, but then surely it had to go some way to…

And then all the excitement drained for her. *And how precisely,* Caroline thought dully, *could I bring myself to marry Stuart when I would always wonder whether he only agreed to it because my dowry was so much more impressive?*

"Miss Caroline?"

The door had opened without either of them noticing. Mrs. Castle stood, looking a little nervous about interrupting. The door to the drawing room was also open, and Caroline could see Jemima and Hugh peering curiously at them.

She could hardly think for excitement. It was all going to be well—that was, if she could find Stuart and persuade him to propose to her again…

"Yes, Mrs. Castle?" her father said abruptly.

Mrs. Castle continued in hushed tones. "There's a gentleman to see you, Miss Caroline."

Caroline stared, confused. "A *gentleman?*"

Wild thoughts rushed through her mind. *A gentleman? Here, now?* But who could it—

Their housekeeper nodded. "Two gentlemen in fact, Miss Caroline, at the door. They say they won't go until they have spoken to you, they are most persistent. I would not want to bother you, not on Christmas Day, but I thought if it was only charity they were after, we could give them some hot cakes I've made special for the poor, and then they could go away."

Caroline stared at Mrs. Castle, who started to go pink.

"But I will ask them to go," she said softly, backing out of the room. "Do not trouble yourself, Miss Caroline, I do not wish to—"

"No, I can go," Caroline said, almost automatically, and she had reached the hall when a hand placed itself gently on her shoulder, and she turned to see…Jemima?

"I will go for you, Caroline," said her stepsister gently. "I do not mind."

Tears welled in Caroline's eyes. Captain Rotherham was clearly some sort of magical cure, for she had never seen Jemima examine her with such sisterly affection.

"I thank you," she managed to say. "No, truly, I do thank you, Jemima. But I do not mind."

How could she mind anything now, when her future had been secured! Thirty thousand pounds! Oh, if only her father had told her before—but what did that matter, now that she knew?

The front door was shut, just as Mrs. Castle liked it, to keep the heat in. Caroline took a deep breath, dashed the few tears which had managed to escape her eyes, and pulled open the front door.

"Good morning, Caroline," said Stuart, "and merry Christmas."

He spoke softly. Both he and the man beside him wore large greatcoats with scarves. The snow which had fallen in the night was thick, and their breath swelled from their noses into the crisp morning breeze. A thin layer of falling snow had settled on their top hats.

Caroline's mouth fell open. "Stuart!"

Stuart smiled nervously.

"I…what are you doing here?" Caroline put her hand on the doorframe to steady herself, unsure whether she could stand without its support. She glanced at her feet, watching the snow swirl onto the door step, then forced her gaze to rise. "You are the last person I would have…yet you are here—and with a friend, I beg your pardon, sir, I do not know you."

The gentleman standing beside Stuart was portly, a little shy of sixty if she was any judge. Despite the cold weather and her less than warm welcome, there was a broad smile on his face.

"Charles Manners-Sutton," he said in a deep rich voice as he bowed.

Already Caroline had forgotten his name, her mind swirling with questions. *Why was Stuart here?* Had he spoken to her father, as she had? But surely it was not possible for a note to have reached him, even if her father had sent it immediately?

So did that mean…

And then something in her mind clicked. *Charles Manners-Sutton.* She knew that name.

But it couldn't be. He wouldn't be here. *This was madness!*

"I beg your pardon," she said weakly. "Did you say—"

"Caroline," interrupted Stuart, "I have something very important to ask you, and I want to ask you quickly."

"But Stuart," said Caroline, raising a finger to point at his companion. "This gentleman is—"

"Yes, I know," Stuart spoke dismissively, not taking his gaze from her. "He's the Archbishop of Canterbury, but that's not what is important right now."

"It certainly is not," Archbishop Manners-Sutton said, nodding with a smile.

"Right," said Caroline weakly. *This was a dream, surely.* "And exactly *what* is important, may I ask?"

"This." Stuart uttered one word before dropping to his knees, paying no heed to the snow soaking through his breeches. "And this."

One hand was thrust into a pocket of his greatcoat and it emerged holding a box—a box Caroline recognized, a blue velvet box.

"And lastly, this." Stuart's other hand opened, and it held a piece of paper covered in writing, along with some rather impressive seals at the bottom.

It was as though the sound of the world had been turned off. All Caroline could do was stare at Stuart, his eyes gazing into hers as if he hoped he could see right into her soul.

The ring. The Archbishop of Canterbury. A rather complex looking legal document?

What was he thinking?

"Stuart, I don't understand," said Caroline helplessly. "Not three days ago you left this house knowing—"

"Knowing?" Stuart shook his head as he opened up the box, the sparkling diamond ring glittering. "The only thing I know is that I love you, and to go through life without you as Dr.

Walsingham or as the fifteenth Earl of Cheshire is no life at all. It is an empty life, bereft of happiness, with no sense. That is all I know."

"But, Stuart," Caroline could not help but whisper, heart singing. "Your mother—the earldom, and the debt! The ultimatum, the thousands upon thousands of people that depend on you…and the thousands upon thousands," she said with a grin she hoped was not too obvious, "I do not have to give you."

"I don't care," said Stuart simply. "I just want you."

There was a small crowd gathering now on the street where the Fitzroys lived, neighbors curious to know whether the kneeling gentleman would be accepted by the woman standing in the doorway—but their presence did not make Caroline hesitate, not even for one moment.

Caroline reached down, pulled Stuart up by the scruff of his scarf, and kissed him passionately with no thought as to spectators.

This was where she belonged. This was exactly what she should have been doing all day, and no one was going to take him from her.

Not this time.

"Put this on," Stuart pulled away as he took the diamond engagement ring from its box, "and never take it off again."

It felt so right. Caroline could not help but beam as she looked first at it, then at him. "Never allow me to walk out of a door like that again, Stuart Walsingham."

The pressure of his lips on hers, his arms wrapped around her—this was agony and ecstasy, and she never wanted to lose him again.

And now, thanks to her father's revelation, she never had to.

"Ahem…"

The gentle cough behind Stuart was the only thing which could make them halt their passionate embrace. A flush of embarrassment filled Caroline's cheeks as she relinquished her grip.

But Archbishop Manners-Sutton was smiling. "I think it is time to fill out the duties of that piece of paper, don't you, Cheshire?"

"You are quite right," said Stuart smoothly, as if he had been referred to by his rank all his life. "Let's get into the warm."

"But I must tell you—" Caroline's protests went unheeded as both men pushed into the warm house, and Archbishop Manners-Sutton closed the door with some relief.

"Now then, to business," he said gruffly. "Let's start by—"

"Who are you?" Her Papa was standing in the hallway, and Caroline could see he was not happy. *Ah.* She had some explaining to do. "And why are you here, young Walsingham? You are not welcome, and you should know that before you take one more step into my house."

"Mr. Fitzroy," said Stuart penitently, moving in front of Caroline. "I can explain—"

"The devil you can!" spat Arthur. A thrill rushed up Caroline's spine; it was rather wonderful to know one's Papa would stand by one, even in the darkest of times. Even though it was, of course, now unnecessary. "You think you can just storm in here with your country parson and expect forgiveness?"

Caroline gasped as she saw Archbishop Manners-Sutton remove his greatcoat and reveal his priestly robes. *Oh Lord, had her father mistaken him for a mere vicar?*

Trying not to laugh, she stepped out from behind Stuart and raised a placating hand. "Papa, it is quite alright, Stuart and I—"

"Oh, it is Stuart again now, is it?" Her father's loud and commanding voice had already summoned the rest of the family from the room.

They were all now clustered in the hall, with Captain Rotherham looking particularly perplexed. Caroline tried not to laugh. This would surely go down in the family history as the most ridiculous—

"Well, I have never claimed to be able to follow you girls and your changes of opinion, but I would have thought that—"

"I will marry you, Caroline," said Stuart quickly. "And find some other way to pay the debt—my mother will no longer stand between us."

There was a moment of silence, in which Caroline turned to stare. *He could not have said…*

"You will?" she said in a whisper, wonder in her voice. "I mean, can you?"

"My mother gave me an ultimatum," Stuart spoke partially to Caroline, partially to her father, and in a way to anyone else who was listening.

Archbishop Manners-Sutton, on the other hand, had joined Sophia on the bench in the hallway. They appeared to be sharing the roasted chestnuts, looking up agog at the entertainment.

"The ultimatum was a choice between my duty and the woman I wanted to become my family," said Stuart simply. "And I don't believe it has to be that clear cut. I will find a way to clear the debts. Caroline is my future, and I am ashamed to say it took until yesterday for me to realize that without her, my life had no purpose."

"But Stuart," Caroline spoke without even thinking, trying not to beam with happiness. *Oh, it was all so perfect!* "I need to tell you, the debt, the money you need to raise—"

"Someone very wise once told me," said Stuart, a smile on his lips, "that you are worth more than any earldom, and they were right."

"Sounds like a damned clever fellow," muttered her Papa, the rage taken out of his voice as he watched his daughter.

Caroline was grinning. "I can't believe you remember that, word for word."

"Everything you say has such weight with me," said Stuart gently. "I very much want to marry you and be your husband, so you can correct me for the rest of my life."

Caroline laughed, and pulling him into her embrace, whispered, "Of course I will—on both counts."

Cheers could be heard from her sisters, and Archbishop Manners-Sutton said in a loud voice, "Bravo that man!"

Her father blinked at the stranger as though he had completely forgotten he was there. "I am sorry, sir—I feel as though I recognize you, but I cannot quite put the face to the name. Are you perhaps a reverend at St. Paul's?"

Rising to his feet, the newcomer said, "Charles Manners-Sutton, my good man, Archbishop of Canterbury. I trespass on your hospitality as a favor to young Cheshire here."

Caroline swallowed. if only she could find a moment alone with Stuart, she needed to tell him—

"A favor?" Caroline's mother was standing with Arabella as they watched the drama play out. "What kind of a favor? Archbishop of Canterbury?"

"This," said Stuart as he held up the piece of paper. "This is a special license, allowing an archbishop to marry us."

Caroline stared, confusion on her face. "Marry us?"

Stuart nodded.

"When?" Caroline still could not comprehend. "Where?"

"Right now," said Stuart softly. "Right here. We do not need to wait for banns, or special announcements—we do not even need to be in a church, if that is what you wish."

Caroline continued to stare, amazed. "I had no idea such a license existed!"

"It doesn't," said Archbishop Manners-Sutton. "Not exactly, it's like the special license but a little more grand, I had to create it specially. I'm thinking of calling it the Cheshire License, but I haven't decided yet."

Laughing, hardly able to believe it, Caroline said, "You cannot be in earnest, Stuart! Now, today, here?"

"I have never been more serious about anything in my life," he said, pulling her close once more and leaning into her so that their noses were almost touching. "I want to marry you, and I do not want to have to wait any longer."

"I shall have to send another letter to Esther and Lucy," said Caroline's Papa behind her. "You never know, it may arrive before the one announcing Jemima's engagement!"

At the same time, her mother protested, "Marry right now? Here, in our hallway? You must be jesting, Stuart, you simply cannot!"

"You know, I think Mama's right," said Sophia. Heads turned to look at the young girl, who was still munching one of the last roasted chestnuts. "After all, you're the fifteenth Earl of Cheshire, isn't that right, Stuart? And you should have a proper party and celebration for your wedding, especially for Caroline. It's what she deserves—what you both deserve."

"Yes, we need another ball!" Jemima said with a smile, Captain Rotherham's arm around her waist. "Another excuse to dance is exactly what we need."

"Dance?" Captain Rotherham's voice was half jesting, half serious. "You are not going to make me do that again, are you?"

"Oh, I love a ball!" Their Mama clapped her hands together. "And it need not be a large one, Stuart, if you do not wish it—we just need to find a room that can host a set of ten, ten dancers and their partners feels about right to me—perhaps now we have another ten lords, now my son-in-law is an earl!"

Stuart chuckled as the noise of the Fitzroys washed over them, Caroline clasped to his side. "Well, we will have to—"

Precisely what they had to do was lost under the noise of a rap on the door. All eyes turned to it.

"Not another one," said their father weakly. "Very well girls, own up—which of you has a suitor behind that door?"

Sophia snorted with laughter, but Arabella flushed. "I-I don't know what you—"

"I'll get it, I'll—oh." Mrs. Castle had left the kitchen to answer the door and was evidently astonished to find the entire family still in the hallway, along with two interlopers. "The door?"

Caroline was nearest. Heart still thundering wildly in excitement for what she still had to reveal to Stuart, she opened the door with a smile on her face. It instantly vanished as she saw the two people on the door step.

"Mrs. Walsingham," she said softly, her heart sinking. "Miss Walsingham. Well. Happy Christmas."

Stuart's mother had a most haughty expression on her face, while Victoria looked merely embarrassed.

"Miss Fitzroy," said Mrs. Walsingham stiffly.

Caroline's stomach dropped.

How long had her happiness lasted—almost five minutes?

She could not be permitted a full hour of joy, it seemed. Stuart's mother had evidently caught wind of his plan and had rushed over to forbid the marriage.

Little did she know that she no longer had any need to…

"Mother?" Stuart had joined Caroline, his voice cold and aloof. "I did not expect you."

Caroline swallowed. This was not the place nor time she had expected to have this conversation.

"Why don't the rest of us go into the drawing room?" came her mother's voice quietly. "My lord, do you like roasted chestnuts?"

"I admit I have consumed them all, my dear lady." The archbishop's voice grew fainter as they left the hallway. "But if you happen to have any more…"

Only she and Stuart remained in the hallway, looking out at his family. *Why had they come?*

"Come inside," Caroline said gently. "You'll freeze out there."

With the door closed behind the two Walsingham women, Caroline took a deep breath and turned to face the woman who had attempted to forbid her happiness.

"Mrs. Walsingham," she said firmly, trying to look her in the eyes. "I—"

"I was wrong."

Caroline blinked. It was so opposite to what she expected Mabel Walsingham to say, the world tipped for a moment to one side.

"I beg your pardon?" asked Stuart quietly.

His mother took a deep breath. "I was wrong. An ultimatum...I should never have considered it."

"That's what I said to begin with," said Victoria with a wry smile. "Why, I told her—"

"But the money, the debt," said Stuart quietly. Caroline looked between him and his mother, and quickly realized this was not a conversation to interrupt. Even if she had the answer to their problems. "All those people who depend on the earldom to survive!"

"We have always been poor," said his mother. "Always. And we have survived. We know how to live on almost nothing, we know how to find ways to—"

Caroline swallowed. It did not seem to be an adequate response to the situation, and it did not appear Stuart thought so either.

"I know we have always been poor, Mother," he said quietly. "Why do you think I came to London in the first place? Why, we had my benefactor then, Great Uncle Edward, though I did not know it. He is gone—blast, some of the debt he accrued was on my behalf!"

Mrs. Walsingham waved aside his words. "No, no, you do not understand me. I mean, we have learned to survive despite having almost no wealth. Earls? They think only of spending. We understand surviving on nothing."

A smile started to curl Caroline's lips. *Oh, this was too perfect.* "You mean...retrench?"

Mrs. Walsingham gave Caroline a rare smile. "Who needs to throw extravagant house parties that last months? Who needs to spend weeks abroad, or days attempting to keep up with the royal family?"

"We certainly cannot afford to," Stuart reminded her. There was still a dark look on his face.

Caroline let out the breath in her lungs, the tension in her temples disappearing. "Do you not see, Stuart, what your mother is saying? We keep on the people—the servants, the farmers, everyone keeps their livelihoods. But we do not spend to excess. We do not drive up more debt, and better—"

"We pay it off," said Stuart's mother triumphantly. "It will take a while, of course. Rome was not paid for in a day."

"It might be a good moment," Caroline said, "for me to mention my dowry."

Mrs. Walsingham waved a hand. "Yes, yes, three thousand is a good place to start of course, but—"

"Not three thousand," said Caroline, ignoring her future mother-in-law, her eyes only for Stuart. "It was what I was going to tell you, before—well, I had a conversation with my father. Apparently, his investments have far exceeded their expectations. I am now worth not three thousand pounds...but thirty thousand."

A rush of delight soared through her as she watched Stuart's jaw drop.

"Thirty—thirty thousand?"

"There or there abouts," Caroline replied cheerfully. "Of course, we may decide to invest some of it, not immediately use it to pay off the debt—I wondered whether—"

"But this...this changes everything," Stuart said, eyes wide. "This—oh, Caroline! We will have years now to sort this all out!"

"A lifetime, perhaps," said Caroline with a wry smile. "Our duty to the earldom, to leave it in a better state—a *solvent* state—for our children."

Stuart's gaze met her eyes, and understanding shot between them. *Their children.*

"I am sorry, child," said Mrs. Walsingham brusquely. "I should never have...I am a difficult woman to love, you will discover that. But you will forgive me?"

Caroline beamed. Nothing could quell her happiness with Stuart by her side. "Of course. Of course—and I am sure, with the right explanation, my parents will be happy to host you for Christmas."

"Do I smell chestnuts roasting?" asked Victoria, sniffing hopefully.

Stuart snorted. "Trust you to follow your stomach. Why don't you take Mother into the drawing room? We'll join you shortly."

It all felt like rather a dream, Caroline thought, as her future mother-in-law and sister-in-law traipsed out of the hall, leaving her alone with Stuart.

He blew out his cheeks. "By Jove. I am not sure what has shocked me more, your fabulous wealth or my mother apologizing."

"Now that," Caroline said dryly, "I did not expect."

"Even so, your dowry will not solve all problems—remember, that fifty thousand was just to pay off the most pressing debts. It would mean living unlike any other earl," Stuart said, taking her hands in hers. "I wouldn't be able to offer you all the jewels and opera visits a countess would expect."

Caroline's heart was singing. *It was a Christmas miracle, everything she wanted.* "You think I want that? You think I wish to leave everything I've known and be holed up in a huge manor somewhere far from our friends and family, so big we cannot afford to heat it?"

"We could rent it out. Let it to a foreign prince, perhaps."

"Take small rooms here," said Caroline enthusiastically. "Stay close to my family."

"As long as I have you," he said quietly, "I do not care what we do."

"Well," she said with a mischievous look, "there are some things on our wedding day—and wedding night—that I think I shall demand we do. But first, we need to plan our wedding ball."

Stuart groaned. "Your mother's ten lords a leaping. Fine. But first…everyone thinks we are discussing financial plans. They will probably leave us alone…"

Caroline raised an eyebrow. "Which means they will not think to look for us upstairs…"

About Emily E K Murdoch

If you love falling in love, then you've come to the right place.

I am a historian and writer and have a varied career to date: from examining medieval manuscripts to designing museum exhibitions, to working as a researcher for the BBC to working for the National Trust.

My books range from England 1050 to Texas 1848, and I can't wait for you to fall in love with my heroes and heroines!

Follow me on twitter and instagram @emilyekmurdoch, find me on facebook at facebook.com/theemilyekmurdoch, and read my blog at www.emilyekmurdoch.com.